Learning to fight

"Where were you?" Flæd demanded when she reached the scriptorium entrance.

"Went to see the smith," Red replied mysteriously. "Follow me." After a second's pause, Flæd hurried after the Mercian envoy, who strode on until they had passed through the gates of the burgh wall. Here he turned and went along the wall until they reached an outcropping at the base of a watch shelter. No guards had been posted here yet, and the place looked deserted to Flæd as she watched her warder poke among the piled stones. He drew out a battered sword of medium length, a leather cap not unlike the one he himself often wore, and a heap of grey metal links which, when held up, proved to be a boy-size shirt of ring mail.

"I told the smith these were for the king's child. He thought I meant Edward," Red told Flæd, "but they will fit you. Let's get started." With a grin Flæd wedged the parchment she had been carrying into a niche of the wall, and began pulling the heavy mail shirt over her tunic.

❧

"A compelling coming-of-age-story . . . Tingle has imagined an action-packed life for Æthelflæd."

—BCCB

OTHER SPEAK BOOKS

The Edge on the Sword

REBECCA TINGLE

speak

An Imprint of Penguin Group (USA) Inc.

SPEAK
Published by Penguin Group
Penguin Group (USA) Inc.,
345 Hudson Street, New York, New York 10014, U.S.A.
Penguin Books Ltd, 80 Strand, London WC2R ORL, England
Penguin Books Australia Ltd,
250 Camberwell Road, Camberwell, Victoria 3124, Australia
Penguin Books Canada Ltd, 10 Alcorn Avenue,
Toronto, Ontario, Canada M4V 3B2
Penguin Books (N.Z.) Ltd, 182-190 Wairau Road, Auckland 10, New Zealand

First published in the United States of America by G. P. Putnam's Sons,
a division of Penguin Putnam Books for Young Readers, 2001
Published by Speak, an imprint of Penguin Group (USA) Inc., 2003

3 5 7 9 10 8 6 4 2

Copyright © Rebecca Tingle, 2001
Map illustration copyright © Karen Savary
All rights reserved

Text set in Aldus.

THE LIBRARY OF CONGRESS HAS CATALOGED
THE G. P. PUTNAM'S SONS EDITION AS FOLLOWS:
Tingle, Rebecca. The edge on the sword / by Rebecca Tingle.
p.   cm. Summary: In ninth-century Britain, fifteen-year-old Æthelflæd,
daughter of King Alfred of West Saxony, finds she must assume new responsibilities much sooner than expected when she is betrothed to Ethelred of
Mercia in order to strengthen a strategic alliance against the Danes.
1. Ethelfled, d. 918—Juvenile fiction.
2. Great Britain—History—Alfred, 871-899—Juvenile fiction.
[1. Ethelfled, d. 918—Fiction. 2. Great Britain—History—Alfred, 871-899—
Fiction. 3. Kings, queens, rulers, etc.—Fiction. 4. Anglo-Saxons—Fiction.
5. Vikings—Fiction. 6. Mercia (Kingdom)—Fiction.] I. Title.
PZ7.T4888 Ed 2001   [Fic]—dc21 00-055353 ISBN 0-399-23580-9

Speak ISBN 0-14-250058-5

Printed in the United States of America

For Bryce,
mannum mildust ond mon ð wærust,
leodum li ð ost ond lofgeornost.

Contents

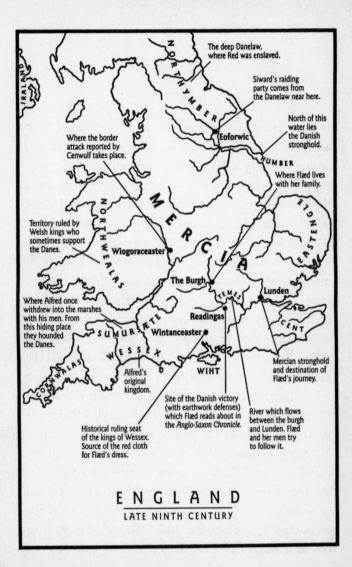

IRALAND

NORTHYMBER

The deep Danelaw, where Red was enslaved.

Siward's raiding party comes from the Danelaw near here.

North of this water lies the Danish stronghold.

Eoforwic

HUMBER

Where the border attack reported by Cenwulf takes place.

Where Flæd lives with her family.

MERCIA

EASTENGLE

Territory ruled by Welsh kings who sometimes support the Danes.

NORTHWEALAS

Wiogoraceaster

The Burgh

Lunden

TEMES

CENT

Where Alfred once withdrew into the marshes with his men. From this hiding place they hounded the Danes.

SUMURSÆTE

Readingas

WESSEX

Wintanceaster

CORNWALAS

Alfred's original kingdom.

WIHT

Mercian stronghold and destination of Flæd's journey.

Historical ruling seat of the kings of Wessex. Source of the red cloth for Flæd's dress.

Site of the Danish victory (with earthwork defenses) which Flæd reads about in the *Anglo-Saxon Chronicle*.

River which flows between the burgh and Lunden. Flæd and her men try to follow it.

ENGLAND
LATE NINTH CENTURY

Note

IN THIS STORY, I HAVE USED THE REAL NAMES OF CERTAIN CHARacters who actually existed in the late ninth and early tenth century. Writing such names is not always easy, because although the Anglo-Saxons of this time mainly wrote using the Roman letters we use today, they also continued to use several much older rune letters. In this story, I have changed the rune letters wyn (ƿ), yogh (ȝ), and thorn (þ) and eth (ð) into the Roman characters w, g, and th, which indicate almost the same consonant sounds to Modern English readers. I have kept one letter, æsc (æ), in its Old English form, in part because there is no good Modern English equivalent, and because it represents the principal sound in my main character's name. The letter æsc (æ) in an Old English word should be pronounced like the short a of our word "cat." So the name "Æthelflæd" rhymes with "apple-glad," and the nickname "Flæd" rhymes with "glad." (As Flæd herself will demonstrate, the name of this letter, æsc, is pronounced "ash.")

The story begins in West Saxony—a kingdom contending with the threat of Danish invaders from the north, with restless and sometimes hostile Welsh neighbors to the west, and with the delicate loyalty of Mercia to the north and the east—a once great kingdom which the West Saxons have just reclaimed from the Danes.

I

Late Winter

1

Dusk

CLUTCHING A GREY CLOAK AROUND HER SHOULDERS, THE GIRL hurried into the broad meadow. The river at the edge of the pasture had flooded with the winter's rain and snow, and had overflowed its banks. Now a shallow lake shone in place of the river's curve, and at the edge of this wetland the girl crouched down to unlace her flat leather shoes. Barefoot, she began to pick her muddy way around the water. Birds rose and landed, calling to each other across the sunset colors of the pool. The girl was shivering by the time she reached the opposite bank of the lake. Quickly she slipped between the first knotted trees of the forest and made her way toward a flicker of light.

She was late. Against her promise, she had kept him waiting. There had been a time, she remembered as she walked the rough path, before promises and arranged meetings. Not so long ago she and her brother had been free to go out together almost every day, the two of them roaming deserted stretches of their father's land. But those days were over now.

Damp branches touched the girl's legs where she had lifted her gown, and scraped across the arm she put up to shield her face. No one had seen her come to the pasture, she felt sure, and so far she had seen no living creature except the birds. She hurried faster, less careful than she had been a few moments before. The light was close now—she was almost there. In her haste, she did not notice a form which slipped from the shadow of a large tree just after she passed and began to follow her along the trail.

A fire brightened the little clearing as she entered it. With a sigh she threw down her shoes and went toward the warmth. Seated in the firelight, another slight figure wrapped in grey wool gave a startled cry and scrambled to get up.

"It's me, Edward," the girl said quickly, "it's Flæd."

"I knew it. Wulf and I knew it was you." He pushed back his hood and gave her a pinched smile, looking up from beneath the fringe of soft brown hair across his forehead. Behind him a big dog with a coarse grey coat raised its sharp face in her direction, eyes glowing. "We've been waiting."

"I know. I'm sorry." Flæd came and seated herself beside him, clasping her arms around her knees and leaning against the dog's flank. "Put some more sticks on the fire, Edward." She nudged him with an elbow. "And bring me my shoes. I dropped them over there." She stretched out her legs as he rose, and scrubbed with her palm at the drying streaks of mud. "I'm almost as dirty as you tonight, little brother."

Flæd's shoes landed with a slap by her hip. Squatting down again, Edward poked at the fire, breaking small branches and adding them. "Wulf and I have to hunt," he said gruffly. "We can't sit around all day and stay clean."

"Not many people can." She snaked a finger toward his ribs, and he fell backward with a yelp. "You've lived just thirteen winters," she tried to tease him, "and already you work so hard."

"*You've* only lived fifteen," he scowled, pushing away her hand. "You don't know so much."

Behind them the dog shifted. A growl rumbled through his body, and Flæd twisted around to stare out into the darkness. No movement. No sound, except the noises of the birds settling themselves for the night out in the flooded pasture. What was bothering Wulf? No one saw me come, Flæd thought anxiously, and no one but us knows about this place. At last Wulf heaved his sides in a sigh. He thrust his big head between the two humans and settled his nose on his paws.

Perhaps Wulf didn't like the two of us raising our voices, Flæd reasoned uneasily, drawing her knees up again and pressing her cheek against the grey folds of her cloak. She and Edward hadn't always spoken to each other in such a strained way. Edward had always been shy, but he used to laugh with her, and the two of them used to be comfortable together. That had been before things changed.

The trouble had started when her father decided that Flæd, his oldest child, should begin lessons in reading and writing. "If Flæd likes it," she remembered him saying, "then we'll let Edward try. Perhaps he's old enough to begin lessons, too." On her first day of lessons she had gone nervously to the scriptorium—the stone building where the monks sat to copy and decorate their pages, and where a number of valuable books were kept—brushing past Edward where he waited outside her door.

"Will we go to the meadow today?" her brother had wanted to know, but she had only shrugged, anxious not to keep her tutor waiting.

Abruptly, her daily rambles with Edward had ended. Flæd went to the scriptorium each day, and as days lengthened into weeks, her thoughts of Edward grew more and more wistful. She had not realized on that first morning that she would hardly see her brother anymore, that the beginning of her lessons marked the end of their wandering together. Flæd's hours in the scriptorium were often lonely. Her teacher, Bishop Asser, one of her father's closest advisors, was a busy man who wasted no time. Usually he would leave Flæd as soon as he had assigned the day's exercises. Surrounded by scribes who rarely said a word to her, Flæd would bend to her task. But she learned quickly in her isolation, and soon she was reading entire words and phrases in Latin as well as in English.

Edward himself had not disappeared. He haunted the scriptorium like an uneasy spirit. Often Flæd would catch sight of her brother passing the entrance of the room where she sat, his eyes seeking her out, then shifting away. Sometimes she would find him slouched outside the door when she emerged. Then he might join her as she walked, mumbling a few words about which animals he and Wulf had seen near the marsh that day. Flæd in turn would try to explain some detail of her day's lesson, and although Edward rarely spoke in response to her descriptions of Latin verbs and English poetry, she saw the way he listened to her—his eyes intense, his mouth twisted quizzically.

"Edward is ready to learn letters, too." That was what she told her father the next time he asked about her lessons. He scarcely speaks to anyone but me, and I am rarely with him, she had worried. King Alfred had looked at his daughter thoughtfully, then told her he would send Edward to the scriptorium, as well.

Flæd had a searing memory of the day when her brother met Bishop Asser. On Edward's first morning Asser had sat down briskly beside his new student, taking up a wax tablet and bone stylus. With a deft hand he sketched a pair of letter shapes, explained them to Edward, and told him to make his own copies next to them. He watched, his sharp eyes on the boy who fumbled with the stylus, trying to match his teacher's sure strokes. Again and again Edward's hand wavered, and he tried to smooth the wax with his fingertip and draw the shapes again. The tutor observed a little longer without speaking, then rose with a gracious bow. He would leave Edward to work at the lesson until tomorrow, he said.

Bishop Asser spoke under his breath as he hurried past Flæd's corner. "Not as quick as his sister," he muttered. "No time for teaching a clumsy child."

Embarrassment washed through Flæd's body, hot and awful—she should not have heard those words. She raised her eyes and watched her brother still struggling over his work, scrubbing at the misshapen lines with his fist now in frustration. Did her teacher not understand that this was Edward's first attempt at writing? *If Edward would only go more slowly, a little patience . . .* Flæd came around the table to stand behind the hunched boy, looking over his shoulder at the ruined wax.

"I heard him." Edward looked up at her and she saw the lines of tears on his face. "I can't learn this." He put down the tablet and stylus and blundered off his bench, hurrying to the door of the scriptorium. There Wulf rose like a smudge and thrust his muzzle into Edward's empty hand, following him out toward the meadow.

Alone beside the deserted table, Flæd reached out for Edward's things. Ruined, Flæd thought. What can I do? After a moment she carried the tablet to the low fire burning at one end of the large room. She held it to the heat until the wax melted smooth. Carefully she wrote the letter forms in the confident hand of the teacher, and beside each one she made three imperfect copies. Then she laid the stylus and tablet on Edward's empty bench and returned to her own work.

Flæd's deception had lasted only until the next day, when

Edward dragged himself back to the scriptorium to sit wood-enly in front of his teacher. Soon it was clear that he could not write the letters by himself, and Asser had sighed, holding the shoulder of the boy who would not meet his eye.

"Have you forgotten your skills so soon," he wanted to know, "or do you simply choose not to write?" Edward made no reply. "Your father warned me that I might find you a reluctant student," the bishop continued regretfully. "Yes, he quoted a maxim, I remember. He said, 'A young man must be taught and encouraged until he is tamed.' For now, I suppose you are still too wild for teaching, boy. Come back when you're ready."

With a shake of his head, Asser bent to view Flæd's work. The girl shot a glance at Edward, who returned her look with a scowl of shame and relief, and then disappeared through the door with Wulf.

She had done the wrong thing, Flæd berated herself over and over, by urging Edward into the classroom so soon. And then she had made it worse when she had tried to help. I'll bring him back to the lessons—I'll think of a way, she told herself each day as she trudged to the scriptorium. But any mention of lessons would send Edward scuttling away like an uncovered beetle, back to the trees with his dog. Worst of all, he almost never spoke to her now, only listening when she occasionally found him at mealtimes and spoke softly of a story or a poem she thought he might like.

And yet here he is, she reminded herself there in the

woods as she warmed her bare feet by their little fire. When I whispered that we could meet out here tonight, he came, and he waited for me, even when I was late.

So what should she say now, to put both of them at ease? She could tell him she'd read more from the book that she'd been describing to him for weeks, every time she ran into him in the kitchen and feasting hall. The story had brought a spark of interest to the remote expression her brother always wore. Tonight she had more of the story. She'd waited until her lesson was over, and hidden beneath the window ledge, waiting for the monks to leave. Then she had snatched down the book as soon as they had left.

"Edward," she offered tentatively, "I did read something today, in a certain room full of old books. . . ."

"You read some more of the story?" the boy guessed. In the light of the coals his face showed the dark eyebrows, narrow chin, and serious grey-blue eyes which matched Flæd's. "Yes, you did," he said quickly as he stared back at his sister in the glow. "Tell me, Flæd. I've been waiting for you to read some more."

A smile touched Flæd's grave face. She had chosen the right words, it seemed. Her brother's voice held an undercurrent of eagerness, and he seemed less guarded. "I'll tell you what I read," she said, wanting to draw him out further, "but first you tell me what you remember."

"Everyone lay asleep in the golden hall," Edward said, rocking forward onto his knees, "and there came a monster—a horrible giant. He broke the hall doors and seized two of the sleeping warriors, and he ate them. He cracked their bones and drank their blood!" Edward shuddered happily, making Flæd grimace—she had thought he might remember the blood.

"And I remember some more," the boy went on. "The greatest warrior was waiting there, awake. When the monster reached for another man, the hero grabbed him, and wouldn't let go. The monster had to tear away his own arm to escape."

"And the monster ran out into the dark, weeping and dying," Flæd continued, still eyeing her brother's bright expression. "And back at the hall they hung up his arm for a trophy, and they sang and celebrated. Do you remember that?"

"Yes," said Edward. "But then what, Flæd?" He touched her arm. "What did you read today?"

"All right." Flæd's voice grew low, more threatening. "A giant woman from the marshes creeps to the hall seeking vengeance—the monster's mother." Edward moved a little closer to his sister.

"The monster's mother," he repeated, clenching his teeth.

"The mother seizes one thane from the hall and carries him off to die at her dreadful pool in the marshes. She leaves his head on the shore for the king's men to find. That," Flæd declared, "is her revenge."

"And then?" Edward pressed.

"And then the king summons the hero to him . . . and then I don't know," Flæd admitted. "I heard someone coming into the scriptorium, so I put the book away and crept outside to the meadow. It was getting too dark to see the letters, anyway."

"It's taking you a long time to read this poem," Edward sighed, flopping backward onto the ground.

"And I haven't seen half of it yet," Flæd told him. Her thoughts were moving quickly. Until tonight she had not known just how much pleasure Edward took in this particular story. Nor had she told him that in order to bring him these few lines at a time, she had become a sort of thief. The poem she shared with Edward was part of a large and valuable book, a collection of the English poetry her father loved. Flæd was still a very junior scholar, and the great manuscript was usually forbidden to her, but one day Asser had given her the first lines of one of its poems to copy, and after she had done the work, she had thought of the poem again and again, wanting to read more.

So she had begun reading the poem secretly, studying in her corner until the scriptorium emptied for meals or prayers, and then glancing into the heavy volume's pages to steal the next lines. Edward had snorted when she first repeated a few passages of the poem for him two weeks ago in the feasting hall. No hero could swim for seven days and kill nine water monsters, he had muttered. Several days later when she saw him in the kitchens, she had whispered a description of the giant's attack, but Edward had said nothing at all that time. She hadn't even been certain he was listening.

After that more than a week had passed before Flæd could snatch another glance at the great collection of poetry, which her tutor still had not invited her to touch again. It seemed, however, that all this while Edward had been waiting, remembering what she had told him, and wondering what would happen to the hero next. Tonight he had stayed here in the dark, perhaps even hoping that she might bring a few more words of the poem with her to their secret place. An idea had come to Flæd, but she knew she would have to put it to Edward with great care.

"If you could help me, Edward," she said cautiously, "if both of us were in the scriptorium, watching, we might find more chances to . . . to open the book."

Her brother turned his head away abruptly and scratched with a stick in the firelit dust. "Wulf and I have to hunt," he mumbled from beneath his heavy fringe of hair. "Reading takes too much time."

Flæd lowered her eyes in disappointment. Why should she have expected him to change his mind about coming to lessons just because of a poem he liked? She picked at the edge of her cloak. It had been stupid to mention lessons. Probably Edward would say nothing more to her for the rest of this evening.

A little murmuring sound caught her ear—Edward *was* saying something, very softly. Flæd held her breath. She heard her brother whispering, repeating a line of poetry she had once recited to him, a description of combat: " '. . . when a bloodstained sword cuts through the crest of a helmet in battle . . .' " I'll try one more time, she resolved.

"Look, Edward," she said, smoothing the dust and ash at the edge of the fire with her palm. "This is the first letter of your name." She wrapped her hand around his on the stick he was stabbing into the ground and traced the vertical line and the three horizontal strokes at its top, middle, and lower right side. Startled, her brother let her draw the letter, and sat looking at the completed form. She reached down and brushed it away. "We'll draw it again," she said, and moved his hand and the bit of wood in the same pattern. "Now," she said, "you try making one here." She smoothed a firelit space next to the E.

Edward sat still for a moment. Then he leaned forward and drew the four lines, a little haltingly. "Good," Flæd said, careful not to let her voice reveal surprise. "Do you want to see the other letters of your name?"

Edward nodded without looking at her. To his E she added D W A R D, and laid down the stick. After a pause Edward picked it up and added his own row of letters beneath the ones she had drawn. Imperfect letters, but recognizable.

"Have you . . . have you been thinking about your first lessons?" Flæd asked, hesitating to say the words.

Edward nodded. "But I couldn't remember the shapes without yours." He dropped the stick and hid his fingers in Wulf's long hair.

Flæd sat silent for a moment, thinking. The fire fell in on itself as the wood burned through, sending sparks to glisten among the letters beside it. "A name can be a kind of word-puzzle," she said at last. "A game to play with letters and meanings. Your name has two parts. The first part, E and D, is like the word *ead*. Can you think what that word means?"

"*Ead*," Edward repeated. "*Ead* means happiness, it means to be happy and rich."

"And the second part of your name, W, A, R, and D, is a form of our word *weard*—that means a guardian, a protector. See? Your name makes pictures in my mind. The first picture is of happiness and riches—I imagine a pile of coins saved to buy a new dagger, or a fine bow." Flæd named objects she remembered Edward coveting once as they walked through the marketplace. "And the second picture, *weard*, is of a someone strong and watchful, someone who cares for people who count on him for protection. The two pictures together, they make me think of someone like Father perhaps, a happy and rich guardian of his people."

Edward's eyebrows made a little crease above his nose. "A happy and rich guardian? That's not me."

Flæd shrugged. "A name is sometimes like a riddle," she said. "At first you don't see the sense of it. But you keep thinking about it, and maybe later you start to understand what it really means."

Edward looked at the letters with the sparks dying among them like tiny jewels. "The pictures you describe help the letter shapes mean something to me," he said slowly, "but you're right, my name is a riddle I don't understand yet."

In the fading light the two of them sat for a time without speaking. Beneath Wulf's shaggy coat Edward's finger moved, tracing the forms that still showed on the earth before him.

Flæd watched the smoke winding up into the darkness. She felt almost unreasonably happy at these little signs from her brother. Pulling her cloak close around her, Flæd began to relax for the first time that night. She let her mind wander away from Edward, from the fire which had almost gone out, to the dog whose rough fur warmed her back. Wulf. She stroked the beard of wiry hairs beneath his chin. He was still alert, she could see, with his ears swiveled back toward the forest behind them.

For the second time since she had reached the clearing, Flæd turned to stare into the woods beyond the dim firelight. What was that? For a moment she had almost believed that one of the forest's shadows, a shape darker than the others, had moved furtively out in the blackness. Narrowing her eyes, Flæd strained to see, but no shape appeared again. Nothing, it was nothing, she soothed herself. Just the story and its monsters, making me nervous.

2

Moonrise

"EDWARD." FLÆD SUDDENLY SHOOK HER BROTHER. "LISTEN! The birds on the meadow lake have gone to sleep. We've stayed too late."

Quickly the two of them buried the coals with handfuls of earth, and the letters of Edward's name disappeared between their fingers. Flæd laced her shoes onto her dusty feet and pulled her hood forward as she followed Edward and Wulf out of the clearing. She turned to peer behind them once, but in the shifting patterns of the wood, she could see nothing unusual. When Wulf lagged, raising his nose to test the air, Edward tugged at his collar.

"No rabbits," Edward told him. "We're in a hurry." Yes, it had probably been nothing more than that, Flæd decided. They circled the meadow, keeping to a route among the trees.

To the east the moon was rising. It poured its light across the black lake, waking some of the birds who grated sleepily to each other. Streaking her imagination with silver, the moonlight twined among the figures in Flæd's mind. It

chased the poem's monsters and the night's odd shadows
into a back corner. It played among the letters of Edward's
name, glinting on their straight lines. It found another word,
and ran its silver fingers curiously over the different sym-
bols. "Æthelflæd," the girl whispered, saying her own full
name. My name-riddle, she thought. The first part, *æthel*,
meant noble and good. *Flæd*, that sounded something like
the word for flowing water, *flod*—it could mean the sea, or
a river. A noble river? I am like Edward, she decided. My
name seems strange to me.

Flæd and Edward left the trees and crossed an open space
before they slipped through a gap in the partly finished stone
wall that surrounded the settlement. Their father, Alfred,
had planned this burgh with broad, unpaved streets, and as
Flæd and Edward stepped into the road that ringed the settlement just inside the defensive wall, they could see that it
was a quiet night. Only a few of the burgh's people were out
along the settlement's main way.

The brother and sister ducked quickly into a parallel
street—one which would take them to the burgh's center
without passing directly in front of the abbey. Alone, they
stole along this less public route, keeping a little distance between themselves and the abbey's stone chapel, scriptorium,
and adjoining dwelling places for the religious orders. Soon,
as they passed thatched wooden dwelling places and the
shuttered workshops of craftspeople, Flæd could make out

the bulky outline of the great hall, around which her family's own group of buildings clustered.

"Flæd," Edward said in a small voice as the two of them scuttled around the sunken, mud-daubed huts of the empty marketplace, "they will be angry with us for being out so late alone and for missing prayers."

"We were careless." Flæd lifted her chin resolutely in the shadow of her hood. "We deserve their anger . . . if they find out," she added.

"Wulf would have protected you," Edward said with dignity.

Flæd smiled. "And you would have protected both of us— our good guardian. Now hurry!" The time for prayers had long since ended, and sounds of conversation flowed out with the soft glow of rushlight spilling through doorways. "Run to the kitchens and find something for yourself and Wulf to eat," Flæd told him. "They might not realize you weren't back earlier."

"You come with us, Flæd," Edward said. "Aren't you hungry?" Flæd felt herself warming with happiness again. This was something Edward would have said before their long weeks apart. But she could not join him tonight.

"Mother expects me, and I'm already late." She pushed him gently between the shoulder blades. "Go on, Edward. You can creep in like the monsters, and run away with what you want."

Edward turned in mock annoyance. "I will walk in like a warrior, a hunter warrior who *asks* for food for himself. And for his companions," he added to Wulf skulking beside him. Flæd smiled again as she watched the pair go off among the royal family's buildings in the direction of the kitchens. By habit they veered into the shadows as they turned to skirt the great hall.

He will probably creep, after all, thought Flæd to herself, shaking her head as she started for her mother's quarters. Strange, solitary Edward. And strange, solitary me, she added. Years of wandering with her brother had left her little inclined to find other acquaintances in the burgh. She had no friends outside her family members, she acknowledged glumly to herself, and now that lessons filled her days, she scarcely even spent time with them.

If at that moment Flæd had looked back one last time, she might have seen a slinking shape that was neither her brother nor Wulf. The figure had drawn much closer after the dog turned aside to go with the boy. But Flæd did not look back.

Moonlight fell around her as she, too, crossed the empty street. It touched the round silver brooch which fastened the grey cloak at Flæd's neck, making the jewelry shine whitely like a tiny copy of the disk in the sky. Flæd was tall, with long legs and thin arms. She walked without clinging to the burgh's concealing angles as her brother had done, but she held her wraps close and let her shoulders slope together, neither awkward nor graceful. In a few steps, like Edward, she had reached the group of spacious, single-roomed structures where her family lived. Silently she entered the passageway which ran between the king's council chamber and the buildings made to shelter the queen and the royal children.

Home, Flæd thought as she halted at her mother's threshold. To her right stood the thatched quarters she shared with her sisters; to the left was the boy's hut—the building where Edward slept with little Æthelweard, the youngest child. Between the children's chambers rose the fine wooden dwelling her father had made for the comfort of his queen. Flæd stood there outside her mother's door, chewing one finger. Edward was right—I'm hungry, she realized as her stomach gave a twist. I should have run to the kitchens with him. A pair of royal guards sauntered into the street from the great hall's entrance, picking their teeth after the evening meal and hailing Flæd as they passed. She considered dashing into the hall to claim her supper. Too many people would notice her, and might wonder where she had been, she concluded. And she had kept her mother waiting too long already. At last she shook back her hood and entered the queen's chamber.

"Flæd, you've come so late." Queen Ealhswith straightened beside the loom frame where she had been kneeling. She pushed back a loose strand of pale hair from her face. "And you're very dusty," she added, as her daughter unfastened her cloak. "Go wash, and then come help me hang the warp."

Without a word, Flæd went to scrub her hands and face at the nearby clay basin. She considered the mud she had tried to brush from her legs by firelight. Her undergown nearly reached her feet, and she still wore her shoes. That grime could wait, she decided, joining her mother at the wooden frame which leaned against the wall.

Vertical threads, called the warp, hung from the top of the loom toward the floor. Her mother's tall form was bent over to fasten red clay rings to the ends of these fine woolen strands, weighting them to hang straight toward the ground against the horizontal weft threads that would be woven across them.

"Look at this fine spinning," her mother said as Flæd knelt beside her and combed her fingers among the hanging filaments to separate them. "It will make a flannel as thick as the stuff of that dustcloud cloak you brought in." Flæd's cloak and Edward's matching one had come from this loom in their mother's quiet room.

Flæd nodded. She had not wanted to speak as she absorbed the warmth of her mother's room, and felt the calm order of the task in front of them. Now she preserved that silence as together they bunched neat handfuls of thread and tied them to the remaining rings.

"There, that's finished," said Ealhswith, securing the last weight. She stood, smoothing the folds of her plain gown, and surveyed her daughter again. "You came straight from the trees, didn't you?" she asked, removing a twig from

Flæd's thick brown hair. "And missed your supper?" Flæd nodded again. "Have a bowl of milk then, and let me untangle that horsetail hanging down your back."

From her mother's hands, Flæd took a carved wooden bowl. The girl sat down beside the little hearth. She inhaled the rich tang of goat's milk as she raised the bowl to her mouth.

"You are very quiet," came Ealhswith's voice behind her. Her fingers loosened the strip of leather binding her daughter's hair. "Tell me where you were tonight."

"I was with Edward at one of our places in the wood," Flæd admitted. "I was telling him a story. We didn't notice how late it was."

"A wild thing, that's what you are sometimes," her mother said, spreading Flæd's hair over her shoulders, "and Edward is wilder." Flæd felt the comb's teeth picking at the tangles low on her back. As a small girl she had loved to hold it and look at the sea animals carved along its handle. Fish played with watery monsters who plunged their strange long bodies in and out of the ivory water. A walrus raised his tusked bulk at each end of the comb, which had once been a walrus's long tooth.

"We only made a fire and sat for a little while," Flæd said.

"You missed evening prayers." Ealhswith lifted a handful of her daughter's hair to her face and sniffed. "The smell of wood smoke will not go." The queen paused, and for a moment she seemed to struggle with some thought. What is it?

Flæd thought. Is Mother so unhappy that I was late? But Ealhswith went on, choosing her words carefully.

"Flæd, you are getting older. Look how tall you are." She straightened Flæd's stooped shoulders gently. "Your father may speak to you about something. . . ."

"About missing prayers tonight?" Flæd blurted. Suddenly her concerns about her brother came rushing to her tongue. "Then shouldn't he speak to Edward, too?" Flæd twisted around to look at her mother. "Edward will be king, and he doesn't know—he doesn't like . . . learning a king's duties."

"Your father should call Edward back to his lessons," her mother agreed, understanding what Flæd was trying to say. "He has thought that Edward should have a little freedom. But now his oldest son must study. And the king will ask his oldest daughter," Ealhswith added, "to take up new responsibilities also." The queen divided Flæd's hair into three sections and began smoothing and plaiting the strands.

A thought passed into Flæd's mind, and she went very still. "You are getting older . . ." Was it possible that her parents had begun to discuss a betrothal for her? But her lessons had only begun—she had just started to see how little she knew, how much more she needed to study. They would not make promises which would take me away from my lessons and away from home, she insisted to herself. Not yet.

"What does my father need me to do?" Flæd asked out loud, slumping down a little and feeling the pull of the plait at the back of her head. She forced her thoughts away from the alarming possibility of betrothal, turning her mind doggedly to her brother again. *I may be the king's first child, but Edward, not I, must prepare to rule after him.* "I might be able to help Edward," she said aloud. "We talk about his reading sometimes. He has a good memory."

"Edward has a quick mind, like yours," her mother agreed as she bound the leather thong around the end of the finished braid. "But Æthelflæd, you have duties, too."

"Edward will be important to all the West Saxon people," Flæd said deliberately, holding her empty bowl on her knees.

"*You* will be important to many people. Flæd," she said, turning her daughter to face her in the lamplight, "I was a Mercian aldorman's child who played in the hills among our sheep. Now I am a queen. A queen who knows how to weave."

What will I be, Flæd wondered, making a face. Probably a weaver who knows how to be a queen. *Could* her mother be warning her to think of her own marriage and the changes such a thing would bring? With hands less sure than they had been a few moments before, she moved to organize the first weft threads.

"No, no, Flæd." The queen gently pushed away her daughter's hands. She gazed at Flæd for a long moment, then seemed to surrender to the girl's reluctance to talk of the future. "Off to sleep with you now." Ealhswith stood with Flæd, embraced her, and went with her to the door. "Take this dusty thing"—she handed Flæd her cloak—"and get to bed."

Ealhswith's shadow stretched out into the street as she watched Flæd go. The girl took only a few steps further along the narrow street to reach the doorway of her own chamber, whose roof nearly touched the thatch of the queen's dwelling. On the threshold of her quarters Flæd glanced again at the queen, who stood still, waiting to see her child step safely inside. She still doesn't like to think of me being alone at night, Flæd thought, her feeling of warmth and comfort creeping back. Pushing aside the cloth which hung across the doorway, Flæd went in.

Another pair of eyes watched the girl step through the doorway, watched the queen retreat to her room. From this vantage point in the shadows between a pile of discarded building stones and the king's council chamber, the watcher reviewed the evening. Several things had become clear. The royal quarters across the little passageway were well attended by serving people, and the narrow street itself was frequented by armed retainers, whose habits would require careful observation. Also, the girl had speed and woodcraft—certain moments tonight had not gone as planned. . . .

But there would be other opportunities, other careless moments. In the darkness by the wall, the figure settled back against the stones to wait.

3

Midnight

QUIETLY FLÆD ENTERED THE ROOMS SHE SHARED WITH HER two younger sisters. Æthelgifu, ten, and Ælfthryth, who had lived eight winters, had been sent to their beds before her. A serving woman waited there, sitting beside a single rush-lamp. Flæd moved silently about the room, which was warm with the slow breath of the sleeping girls. She washed the dirt from her feet and legs and changed her tunic and undergown for a linen shift, pinching dead the lamp before she curled beneath her own blankets.

When she awoke later in the dark, Flæd could hear a faint creaking of boards, as if another wakeful person were pacing back and forth across a wooden floor. Coming from across the way, she decided as she lay there, listening. From Father's council chamber, she thought. Flæd sat up and wound herself in the brown woolen blanket from her bed. Slipping past the serving woman asleep near her door, she padded outside and crossed the narrow street to her father's threshold. The single guard posted there gave her a little bow, and

Flæd stopped to listen again. Yes, there were the sounds of footsteps she had heard. Her father must be awake and walking the length of his room. Putting her palm against the door frame, the girl tapped softly.

"It's Flæd, Father."

"Come in."

At one end of the room candles shone down on a table covered with sheets of parchment, quills, and books in their leather-strung wooden bindings. Her father was just seating himself at the table as she entered. Thin brown hair curled around his long face, softening its bony starkness and mingling with his short beard.

"Flæd, you should be resting."

"I thought I heard you."

Her father sat back, holding out his hand for her to come closer. "Well, it's good you came. I was getting tired of pacing alone," he said, drawing her to a stool beside his chair. "Alone except for these." He gestured wearily toward the piles on the table. "A daughter is far better company than silent pages. Tell me how you passed your day."

And so Flæd told the king how Æthelweard the baby had tried to follow Edward and Wulf to the woods that morning, running on his short legs until his nurse pulled him back. She described how at the noon meal, when her smaller sister, Ælfthryth, had broken a wooden spoon as she beat out a rhythm for a song, pious Æthelgifu (called "Dove" after the holy bird) had tried not to laugh. "And tonight I went across the meadow to meet Edward. I . . . we missed the chapel service. Edward almost missed the evening meal." She bit her lip.

"Your absence was noted," her father said. He gazed at her intently for several seconds, then spoke again. "Flæd, I settled our family not at the largest of our estates, but in this quiet place because I wanted freedom for my children. You have given up some of that freedom, I know, since beginning your lessons. But now a time is coming"—he propped an elbow against the table and let his fingers crease his brow into furrows—"when you, and Edward, too, will have to leave more of your freedoms behind."

Flæd froze. What had her mother said? *"Your father may speak to you about something."* But what exactly did the king mean by *". . . leave more of your freedoms . . ."*? Perhaps—Flæd let the idea loose again, her panic rising—perhaps she had been right before. Maybe she had guessed correctly as she sat in her mother's room, wondering if her parents might be considering betrothal and marriage for their oldest daughter. No, a voice inside her shouted, there must be something else—a blunder Father has discovered, a mistake in my lessons, or my deception of Bishop Asser when Edward was with us. . . . Desperately, she searched for an alternative: her most recent secret, that must be it. He must know she'd touched the valuable book in the scriptorium.

"Please, Father," she burst out, "let me finish the poem

with the monsters and the great hero. The hero will follow them to their lair and—"

Her father's gentle laughter stopped her. "You missed prayers tonight, Flæd, but not confession, I see. If you have been reading our great book of poetry, your lessons are too easy."

No, the king had not known about the manuscript, after all. Head spinning, Flæd tried to respond to what her father had said. In her mind she compared the plain religious passage she had copied that afternoon with the echoing sounds that made the poem beautiful, even when its images were terrible: *Grim and greedy, the death-spirit grasped him.* "Yes, my lessons are too easy," she faltered.

"I wonder if you have heard a story, a true one, about my childhood," her father said. "One afternoon my brothers and I sat with your grandmother queen Osburh, listening to her read English poems from a small and beautiful book. My brothers were restless, so Mother tried to make a game of it. Whoever could learn the book fastest, she said, could have it. I took the book and ran to find our priest. All I could think of was that the book could be mine if . . ." He paused.

"If you could read it quickly enough?" Flæd asked, her mind still churning with uncertainties.

"If someone could read it to me," her father finished. "My father's court was a busy place—the wars already troubled our kingdom—and no one had found time to teach the king's fifth son, his sickly son, to understand writing. This is why I ran to the priest."

"How old were you?"

"Thirteen. Edward's age. The priest helped me memorize the book." His daughter cocked her head. "Mother had said whoever could *learn* the book first could have it. I recited every word. Look." He rummaged among the books and scattered pages on his desk, and drew out a small leather-bound booklet which could be held comfortably in two hands. He passed it to Flæd. "It is not very useful here, but I like to keep it nearby."

She held the soft edges and spine of the fine little book, worn by much handling. "Did you covet the book for its appearance?" she asked doubtfully.

"I might well have loved the look of it," her father said, amused. He took the book from her and opened it on the table between them in the candlelight. Beneath Flæd's eye spread a little mosaic of red and purple and green and gold. Long-bodied animal shapes wove around the gilt lines of a finely drawn initial capital letter which occupied more than a third of the small page. The faces of the colorfully twisting forms peered out at her—she saw a lion's heavy jaw, the rolling eye of a goat beneath a delicate forelock and curling horns. The lines of the letter itself formed a conjoined *A* and *E*.

"It's an *æsc*," Flæd said, pronouncing the name like the

tree, *ash*, from which they took the strong wood to make spears.

"Yes, an *æsc*, the first letter the priest would teach me. The first letter of the first poem in this, my first book. And the first letter of my oldest child's name. The book reminds me how I felt as a boy, how my trickle of interest in a poem could become a flood of learning." The king looked at his daughter with a smile. "A noble flood, Æthelflæd."

Then the king sighed. "But I cannot keep all my precious firsts." He reached out and took her hand. "Before poetry distracted me, we were speaking of new responsibilities. Edward must return from the woods to his schooling. And you, too, must prepare for a change. Flæd, at the end of the summer you will marry Ethelred of Mercia, my friend and ally. Today I have received this acceptance from him."

Flæd sat fixed upon her stool as the king took a sheet of parchment from the table and gave it to her. She hardly felt the page as she took it between her fingers. As she stared at it, instead of seeing the words, she only heard the name her father had pronounced, echoing in her head. *Ethelred of Mercia* . . . a man she had never met. She could put no face to the name. Why now, she wondered dumbly. Why tonight?

A flurry of thoughts passed through Flæd's mind. She found herself grasping at moments of the evening she had just spent with Edward, of other evenings, days, and years spent here at the heart of her family's life together. But she could not keep these scenes in her head—her father's announcement crowded them aside. Of course she had known that after the passing of another season she would be sixteen, a marriageable age. Still, Flæd had never given serious thought to her own betrothal, and she knew almost nothing about Ethelred the chief aldorman of Mercia except that he was the king's friend, a man as old as her father.

Another memory flashed into Flæd's consciousness. Her grandfather had married his second wife, Judith, daughter of the Frankish king, when she was only thirteen. She had been even younger than Alfred when she became his stepmother, taking the place of the mother who had given Alfred the book of poems. Judith the Frankish princess, marrying the widowed West Saxon king with his six adult children. . . .

Flæd's father still held her hand, but she withdrew it now. With unsteady fingers she placed the parchment page on the table between them.

"Flæd?" Alfred's gentle tone made her meet his eyes. "I can no longer allow you to go about alone, even within the boundaries of the estate. There are enemies who would injure this alliance by injuring my daughter."

Still she said nothing. "You will have a personal guardian," she heard her father say, "who will always be with you. You may go to the scriptorium or the kitchens, to the woods or to the chapel, moving wherever you like, but always with this warder. He will sleep by your door. He will watch and keep you safe, always. You are dear to me, and to the West Saxon kingdom. We must not lose you, Æthelflæd."

He stood, and drew her up from the stool, leading her toward the door. "These are heavy things—I am sorry. But tomorrow morning when your guardian arrives, you will understand. I think it was right to tell you now."

Flæd went out, barefoot again in the crumbling dust of the road. The moon made a dwarf girl-image on the ground next to her, and numbly she watched it trudging along with each of her steps. Beside her own doorway Flæd paused: No guardian sat there yet. After a moment she walked on, faster, until she had passed the last of the silent buildings and stood again at the edge of the meadow. The dark water moved a little with the night wind, glinting here and there. Between Flæd and the water lay a narrow strip of unflooded pasture where a group of horses stood with their heads lowered to the grass.

It seemed to Flæd as if a door, heavy and ironbound like the ones at the entrance of her father's great hall, had crashed shut in her face. Edward, her parents, the little ones—she was calling them, pounding against the door, fighting against a man's hands that captured hers and held her, helpless. She had been given in marriage. *"At the end of the summer you will marry Ethelred of Mercia. . . ."* She had been given away. *"You are dear to me. . . ."* She had been given to a man she had never seen.

Run, Flæd spoke in her mind to the black forms in the meadow. "Run," she said to the horses in a whisper. Waking, one horse moved its lips over the short blades of grass in front of its feet, and then was still again. Run! she cried inside herself, but then, slowly, she turned to go back along the road to her father's burgh.

The figure which had followed Flæd to the pasture did not return to the burgh with her. It had been a stroke of luck to see the girl leave her own room in the dead of night. She had come very close to the pile of discarded stones—only the presence of the guard had preserved her then—but even this proved fortunate. Behind the mound of rubble the watcher had pressed an ear to the council chamber wall, the better to hear the conversation between the king and his daughter.

Afterward, even though it had been maddening to leave the girl untouched as she wandered out alone beyond the walls of the burgh, the figure had simply trailed her, knowing that King Alfred's words to his daughter had changed things. Others would need to hear of this new development before any action could be taken. The dark shape crept between the horses, which began to mill about. One, unable to escape, rolled its eyes at the strange rider swinging up onto its back. Practiced hands subdued the horse, and the gallop north began.

4

Red

"That's my shoe!"

"It's too big for you, Ælf. Give it back!"

Jerked out of a shallow sleep, Flæd squeezed her eyes shut as the memory of her father's announcement settled over her again. *"Ethelred of Mercia . . . at the end of the summer . . ."* If she pretended to be asleep, the women who had come to dress her quarreling sisters might take them to prayers and leave her alone. Flæd listened as the argument moved toward the entrance of their chamber. Abruptly, the little girls' voices broke off, and Flæd heard only the pat of leather-shod feet across the wooden floor, and then the soft swish of the cloth hanging as it fell back across the doorway.

They were gone. Flæd opened her eyes and pushed back the blanket, shivering in her linen shift. Rain tapped against the wooden shutters above her bed. It was a dismal day. Had the rain ended her sisters' argument, she wondered listlessly as she sat up.

In the entrance to her room, just inside the heavy fabric

which hung across the door's opening, a man was sitting down on the floor. He leaned back to rest his shoulders heavily against one side of the doorway. Droplets of water had beaded along the short hair above his brow, and one larger drop clung to his nose. Flæd sat frozen among her bedclothes. She watched the man raise a hand to wipe his face. Behind him the weak morning light shone through the cloth, outlining the slumping squareness of his frame, illuminating his blunt facial features and heavy clothing. He showed no sign that he had noticed she was awake. On her threshold he sat and dripped and looked at the damp leather of his boots.

"Tomorrow morning when your guardian arrives, you will understand." Thoughts of her betrothal had overshadowed these words last night, but now the shock of the stranger's presence brought them back. This must be the warder her father had described—his arrival must have silenced her sisters. Flæd felt last night's whisper to the horses batter up inside her again. *Run.*

Instead she sat up and put her feet on the cold wood floor. This time the man in the doorway lifted his head. Flæd kept her eyes on the wall opposite her.

"Stand outside the door," she said stiffly. "I will dress to go out." For a few seconds both of them were still. Then her warder got to his feet again and stepped out into the drizzle.

Flæd found the clothes which the serving women had laid out for her and put them on. Cold water on face. Hands twisting and plaiting hair. Leather shoes bound stiffly onto feet. The attendants had shaken the dust from her cloak and had hung it beside her bed. She wrapped it around her, hunched up her shoulders, and went outside.

Flæd cringed as she stepped out into the rain and hurried past the man standing there. In a moment she was flailing to keep her balance as her feet slipped among wheel ruts and deep, pocklike hoofprints. The edge of her gown grew heavy with mud and slapped against her ankles, and rain ran into the folds of the grey cloak. She ducked inside the kitchen building just as the first trickle ran down her neck.

Flæd accepted a bowlful of porridge from a kitchen worker's hands and found a place by the hearth. He had come in with her again, she saw with a sinking feeling. There he was, in the corner beside the entrance. Flæd watched the man scrutinize each newcomer who entered the room. When his square face turned toward her, she quickly looked away and began to spoon up her porridge. Her guardian was so large he seemed oafish, and he was not young—perhaps as old as forty winters. This was the person who would stalk behind her every day from now on. Everyone would stare at her. Edward's dog would growl. This warder would follow her to chapel, to meals, to her doorstep when she returned to her chamber—how could anyone fail to notice her presence with this great, awkward shadow trailing along with her? Flæd felt a rush of humiliation as she thought about it.

Above the busy sounds of the kitchen came the high, clear

sound of a bell marking the third hour since sunrise, calling the monks to prayer. Flæd stood up with a start. The third hour already? Filled with dread, she began to push her way across the busy room. With a little yelp of frustration she dodged her warder, who had risen and stepped into her path when he saw her coming. At last she reached the doorway and ran out into the street.

The rain was in her hair and on her face again before she could pull up her hood, wetting her cheeks like strange, cold tears. She kept running, sliding in the mud and almost falling, but she didn't care. If she was absent when her lesson was supposed to begin, Asser would go about his other work. She had not been late before, but her father had warned her that she must never keep her teacher waiting. He was a busy man who must never feel unduly burdened with teaching her. Flæd hurried on, fighting back the burn of real tears.

She pushed past the heavy scriptorium door and entered the vaulted room with ragged, echoing breath. Her shoes slopped soggily on the flagstones of the room, and the nearest writers, who were just preparing to leave their work for prayers, edged the corners of their parchment away from her dripping clothes. Flæd skirted the room, looking for her teacher, who usually prayed quickly and came directly here to meet her. Was he late today, just as she was? Her eyes found the shelf where she usually stored her writing tools and gospel primer. Empty. Could Asser have come already and taken away her things when he saw she had not arrived?

Flæd stopped in confusion and despair, tears now brimming in earnest.

"Flæd." Edward's voice sounded over the rustle and murmur of the scriptorium and she jerked her head like a startled animal. "Here, by the window." There sat her brother, peering at her anxiously. Wulf stretched long and calm beneath Edward's bench, his damp black nose dripping. On a stool at the low writing table sat a brown-robed cleric she didn't know. He stood as Flæd tried to smooth her trembling face.

"Lady," he said, inclining his head so that she saw his tonsured scalp, "I am called John. Bishop Asser has suggested that I should teach you for a little while." He was a very young priest, Flæd could see, a round-faced man whose voice was soft and deep. "Your brother and I have brought your things to the table. Will you join us?"

"Where were you?" Edward demanded under his breath as she took her seat at the table and drew her book toward her. "I told him you were never late for our lessons."

"How would you know that? You never attend *our* lessons," Flæd whispered back sharply, feeling baffled and short-tempered. Still shaking from her race across the burgh, she tried to arrange her muddy shoes beneath the table. She took up her wax tablet with one dripping hand and found the last ruled line where her lettering had ended the day before. The new tutor was called John. Father John, she ought to call him. She should try to review yesterday's lesson. John . . . Father John would question her about those verses.

But it was Edward's voice which interrupted her thoughts. He spoke quietly: "Who is that man who came in with you?" Flæd looked up abruptly from her book. "Over there." By the doorway her guardian sat, colorless as the stonework around him. Rainwater had run off his clothes and darkened the floor and wall in the corner where he had placed himself. Flæd ground her palm against the bench in vexation, shivering as the chill of the scriptorium seeped into her wet clothes. Was this how it would be? Would he truly follow her tiniest movement, even into this sanctuary? She ought to talk to her brother alone, tell him about this man and the arrangements the king had made, as soon as they could escape again to their place in the wood. . . .

No. There would be no more escapes with Edward. There would be no more time alone, and at the end of the summer, she would have to leave Edward, her books, everything. That was the meaning of the man in the corner.

Bitterly she turned away from her warder and her brother. The new tutor began speaking, and she tried to focus on her tablet again, preparing for a test of her skills.

But the priest was not talking to her. He was talking with Edward. She watched as their new teacher carefully stroked Wulf's jaw and chest in greeting. The dog looked him clearly in the eye, then looked away, lowering his head to rest on Edward's foot.

"Has he always been in your care?" the tutor asked, and Flæd heard Edward begin to talk about Wulf's puppyhood.

What was happening here? Edward sat, a little disheveled by the rain, cross-legged on his bench. His head was stretched forward from his shoulders like a bird, and although his eyes roved around the walls and windows of the scriptorium restlessly, they sometimes raised to the young priest's face.

Was this the little brother who scarcely spoke to anyone, hardly even to her these days? Edward began to tell John of a special snare he had devised to catch swift game when Wulf was still a puppy. Flæd watched the boy's hands make lines and circles on the tabletop, showing how the trap worked. He showed me that trap when he made it, she thought in consternation, he showed only me. . . . Still nodding, the priest pushed the wax tablet toward Edward's hands. Asking another question, he tapped the tablet with the bone stylus, offering it to Edward and bending over to see the shapes the boy began to draw. He moved away as Edward's words faded and the boy concentrated on making a picture.

"Lady," the priest addressed Flæd softly, performing a little bow, "will you show me the lesson Bishop Asser gave you yesterday?" Tearing her eyes away from her brother, Flæd turned back to her own tablet. In some ways, at least, this new teacher was predictable.

He stayed, unlike Asser, to read Flæd's lesson with her and offer his quiet corrections. Father John's main attention, though, was for Edward, with whom he continued to talk about hunting, about the woods, about Wulf. As she sat with them at the table, Flæd could sense an eagerness in Edward which she only remembered seeing by firelight or moonlight when they were talking alone together. Watching him, she felt confused, and a little dejected. She turned a little to one side and tried not to think about her brother as she wrote out her lesson, making the strokes on her wax match the carefully ruled lines of writing in the book she copied. The book's rulings were measured according to prick marks along the sides of the page, and were scored into the parchment without ink, using only the pressure of a metal stylus. Behind the dark letters the lines seemed to disappear.

I am like those lines, Flæd thought as she worked. Edward hardly sees me, nor does Father John. She was disappearing already, she decided. Even before her betrothal was known to others, she felt herself fading beneath the words of a promise her father had made to another man. Deliberately she continued to fill her tablet.

By the time the bell rang to signal the ninth hour since sunrise, she had finished all the work her new tutor had given her. Outside the sky had cleared. In the slanting afternoon light the scriptorium writers continued working. Edward and the young priest were talking about another drawing Edward had made on the wax tablet.

"Here is the Hunter, high in the west." Edward pointed to the upper left hand portion of his picture, where he had marked the constellation as he and Flæd had seen it last night. "And the Dog here, just south of him." Edward moved his hand slightly to the left of his drawing.

The tutor smiled. "It seems that you and your dog appear in everything you tell or show to me, sir."

"My teacher should call me Edward." Edward flushed. "Wulf and I," he continued with less shyness, "are not the same as the Hunter and his dog. But I can put myself in that picture." At the bottom of the tablet Edward's sketch showed how a tree-lined path followed the edge of a pool which Edward had covered with tiny wave-marks and ripples scratched into the wax. Carefully, beside the pool Edward added a figure in a boy's short tunic and leggings, accompanied by Wulf's shaggy outline. Then beneath the human figure Edward marked a vertical line with three horizontal strokes intersecting it, top, center, and bottom. "That is a drawing of me," he said, looking up at the young priest. "And that is the letter that begins my name, Edward."

"Indeed, that is the first letter," returned the tutor. "Do you know the others?" Edward nodded. "And will you draw them for me next to the E?" Edward bent over the tablet to begin forming the first descending stroke of the letter D.

Across the table from them, Flæd felt a lump rising in her throat. She watched the muscles of her brother's smooth cheek flex in concentration, saw the letters she had taught him appearing on the wax. I wanted him here because I thought he needed other companions, she realized with unexpected bitterness, I wanted this. Flæd reached out to touch the priest's sleeve.

"Please, I have finished," she said in a low voice. "May I go?"

"Of course, Lady." He spoke very quietly, leaning away from the boy. "Until tomorrow, then?" Flæd nodded, and went out past the warder, hearing him rise to his feet behind her with a creaking of leather.

The mud of the morning had turned to a soft clay that took a foot's perfect imprint but left shoes and hooves clean. Flæd walked along a high ridge of earth pushed up to the side of a wheel rut. Men and women passed her carrying bundles of fuel and loads of woolen cloth. People led horses, spoke to each other, prodded small bunches of sheep along the road-way between the wooden buildings of the burgh. But Flæd saw little of this. Her mind lagged behind, thinking of her brother and the new teacher working so comfortably to-gether in the scriptorium. Edward hardly looked at me all day, she brooded. Nor had their new teacher seemed partic-ularly interested in the king's daughter. Only her unwel-come guardian had fixed his attention on her. It wasn't fair.

In her room someone had opened the shutters, and a square of sunlight fell across the coverlet. Flæd sat down in the middle of it, pulling her legs up under her skirts.

Her warder was there of course, settling himself on the stone stoop. The door frame partly covered his face, but Flæd could see the bristling short hairs of his head and beard as he leaned back into the afternoon shadow from the roof. People passing along the street glanced at the stranger as they went—who was this man seated almost inside the chamber of the king's daughters? Flæd curled herself together more tightly. Tonight her father would announce her betrothal, she thought with resignation. Then everyone would know.

In the doorway her warder had begun to clean the dried mud from his boots with a knife. Flæd watched the muscles of his lower arm cord and strain as the knifepoint dug through the caked earth. An unusual grey bracelet was clasped around the wrist of his knife-hand. Made of heavy, ugly metal, it did not seem like a decoration. Neither was it an archer's protective band—it was on the wrong wrist, and it was not broad enough to cover the vulnerable veins and tendons a bowstring or an attacker's weapon might slash. The bracelet glinted a little on his arm as he worked in the shadow. Strange, Flæd thought, unsuitable for this man.

Then, with a chill, Flæd understood what it must be. Her eyes flicked to the man's neck. Yes. Another narrow metal band showed just above the neckline of his heavy leather overtunic. The man wore tokens of slavery.

Disbelief mingled with affront rushed through Flæd's mind. There were slaves among the royal household's servants, as there were in most social circles of the West Saxon kingdom. But rarely were they trusted with the care of very important people. Hadn't her father valued her safety any more than this?

Flæd shut her eyes. I don't understand, she thought miserably. Maybe Father will explain later. Too many things had wounded her today, and she had little strength left for this last indignity. I need to be like a stone, like ice, Flæd told herself doggedly. Edward has someone else now, that's good. I thought he should. And maybe the new teacher already knows I'm going away. Why should he spend much time with a student who will be leaving soon? It wasn't a happy feeling, the numbness that began to replace her hurt, but numbness was all she wanted right now.

The knife scraped on dirt and leather—a mineral, monotonous sound. Flæd lay back on her bed and turned her face away from the doorway where the man sat working over his boot. A few seconds later she spoke over her shoulder.

"What is your name?"

The man looked up at his charge, huddled in her patch of sunlight.

"Red," he said gruffly, and looked away.

In the Great Hall

"WHERE WERE YOU AT THE EVENING SERVICE, FLÆD?"
Æthelgifu demanded. "You haven't been there for two nights
in a row."

"I was here. I didn't feel well." Stonily Flæd drew a long
gown of rust-colored wool over her head, but she felt the ice
inside her begin to soften a little. She knew her sister wanted
her to share in her earnest prayers each evening, but she
was sure that thin Dove also appreciated the warmth of a
larger body kneeling beside her in the frigid chapel.

"You said you would help me make a stick horse today!"
Ælfthryth accused, wriggling away from a woman who
struggled to put a comb to the little girl's wild blond hair.
"You said you would!"

"I did say that, little elf." Now Flæd's composure was
melting away in earnest. She imagined herself for a moment
making the toy for Ælf to ride, fastening dry grass along a
green stick of willow to make a mane, with a tuft of long
rushes at the other end for a tail—all under the watchful

eye of her warder, the man named Red. Flæd hugged the little girl to hide the dismay she suddenly felt. "Tomorrow, I
promise, if the rain stays away, we'll make you a willow
horse."

"Do you know who the guest will be tonight?" Dove
asked. "I've asked everyone, and no one seems to know."

"The only new person around is that man on our
doorstep," Ælf said loudly, and then clapped both hands over
her mouth. The man outside could certainly hear through
the cloth draped across the doorway. "Who is he, Flæd?" she
whispered.

"Hush, little one," Flæd said sadly, turning away from
the serving women's curious glances. "We'll talk about that
another time."

Ælf was cornered by the woman with the comb, and Dove
was led away to see if a blue gown Flæd used to wear might
fit better than the ones she kept outgrowing. Flæd combed
out her own hair with nervous fingers and bound it neatly
again into a single braid. At her shoulder she pinned the silver brooch, wishing she could just stay in this room tonight,
wishing she could curl up on her bed again and try not to
think or feel. "Come," she forced herself to say to her sisters
as she retrieved her cloak from the bed. "I mustn't be late."

The three girls and their attendant women set out for the
hall. Tonight the lowest-ranking servants and laborers would
tend their masters' homes, but everyone else would come to
feast with the king and his family. A few townspeople still

hurried along the street as the royal sisters walked between the shuttered houses. Some of them noticed the silent, bulky guardian following close behind the little company of women and girls.

The great hall was one of the burgh's newest buildings. It was built of the same yellow stone quarried to make the burgh's first church with its adjoining scriptorium, and the partly finished ramparts around the settlement. Eventually the royal family would have a great house of stone as well, but for now Alfred sent all the new blocks to finish the protective wall. The hall was a place of luxury in the heart of the young burgh, with rich cloth-hung walls and a vast open hearth. Heavy beams spanned the high ceilings, where smoke swirled far above the folk gathered at the benches and tables which filled the room. Torchlight and rushlight brightened a guest's view from the entrance all the way to the king's seat at the opposite end of the hall. When he feasted here with his townspeople, Alfred occupied a tall-backed oaken chair carved with twin dragons which wove in and out of each other's coils and then swallowed their own tails. A smoothly polished red gem formed the gleaming eye of each beast.

Noise and warmth rushed to greet the sisters as they entered the hall and walked between the crowded tables toward their father's seat. At the end of the hall the sisters turned aside with their serving women to take their usual places on a bench where Edward, little Æthelweard (held on a servant's lap), and Father John were already seated. With a wave Alfred indicated that Flæd should take the empty seat beside him and Ealhswith. The blood surged in Flæd's cheeks as she walked to join her parents at the raised table.

Luckily, the noisy feasters spared little attention for Flæd. This late winter meal of meat, of round barley loaves, of honey collected in autumn, and of sharply aged cheeses was welcome to the townspeople tired of dull winter fare.

Soon Ealhswith rose and with both hands took from Alfred a broad silver cup of mead. Flæd watched her mother circle the high table where the king's closest retainers and advisors sat, ceremoniously offering the cup to each guest with words of greeting and thanks. Flæd tried to catch Edward's eye, but found him in conversation with the young priest John, who was offering a sliver of meat to Wulf beneath their table. With a pang Flæd turned back to her meal.

"Dear friends of my hearth, and people of this burgh," Alfred called out, rising from his seat. The hall quieted as the king drew breath to continue, and Flæd quickly dropped her eyes, wishing she could hide somewhere. "I welcome you to our hall, to share this meat and bread."

"And mead!" someone shouted out to general laughter, in which Alfred joined.

"You have had your share of it, I think," the king called back. After more laughter the people stilled again. "Many of you, I know, are wondering whom we honor tonight. The first of our honored guests does not boast of his own deeds, although many know his worth. This man asks to be known simply as the envoy. He comes to us from the hearth of Ethelred, my aldorman in Mercia. The envoy would not join us at the high table, but I ask him to accept the cup from Queen Ealhswith, and be welcomed by us today."

Alfred looked toward the far reaches of the hall, where a man stepped from the shadows by the door and came forward to stand near the foot of the king's table. It was Flæd's guardian, still wearing the plain leather clothing which had dried on his back after the rain. Honored guest? Envoy? Flæd felt more bewildered than ever by her new protector. Ealhswith held out the cup, and with a glint of the slave ring on his arm, the man took it from her, drank, and quietly withdrew.

"This envoy has come from Mercia with a message," Alfred continued. "His lord Ethelred has noticed that I have amassed a fine hoard of daughters. I have kept them close to me, Aldorman Ethelred says, like a dragon brooding over his gold." Some laughter again. "But as our maxims tell us, 'The head must influence the hand.' The envoy's message explains that his lord Ethelred of Mercia wishes to marry my daughter Æthelflæd"—there was a low sound of appreciation from the gathered folk. "So," Alfred said with a glance at Flæd, "I am asked to share my child, to give her in marriage to the man who holds Mercia for the West Saxon kingdom. Aldorman Ethelred knows he has asked for a great gift, and he sends his own tribute."

Three serving men of the king's household stepped forward and held up before the crowd a flexible ring of gold which would fit closely around a noblewoman's neck, a belt of linked golden rings like the one Ealhswith wore, and a delicate, twisted band of gold meant to encircle a royal woman's brow. The servants laid them, one by one, in front of Flæd.

"Ethelred has fashioned rich gifts for his bride," Alfred said. "This is shrewd, for she will carry them back to him as ornaments worn by the far greater prize of a noble wife."

Shouts of approval greeted Alfred's speech, and he turned to his daughter, who sat staring at the gifts on the table before her. "The second guest we honor tonight is Æthelflæd, whose marriage will bind English Mercia all the more closely to the West Saxons." There was cheering in the hall, and Flæd turned to find her mother beside her with the silver cup.

"Drink, Flæd," she said softly, "and be honored." Flæd took the heavy vessel in her hands. She looked at her mother, remembering how yesterday Ealhswith had tried to forewarn her of the king's news. There were her two sisters, pointing at Flæd and chattering eagerly to the women beside them. *They don't really understand yet. But Edward ...* Edward sat with lowered head, twisting his fingers in Wulf's fur. *Edward can see what this must mean.* Finally she caught

Alfred's keen gaze—her father was waiting. Flæd brought the cup to her lips and tasted the mead, sweet and stinging on her tongue.

The noise from the hall carried through the burgh to the half-finished outer wall, where the drenched sentries grumbled at their bad luck. Beyond their sight, at the far end of the meadow, a horse newly freed from a bridle shook its head and began trotting around the lake. It would join the herd again unnoticed after its brief absence, and the two new horses which followed close after it would likely graze undiscovered among the other bays and browns of the roving band. Three muffled figures, dusty from a swift journey, watched the horses go, then disappeared noiselessly into the wood.

II
Spring

6

The Marsh

ÆTHELFLÆD WAS CRAWLING ON HER BELLY THROUGH THE MUD.
Brown clay-filled earth sucked at her hands as she pulled
herself along. Her clothing clung to her like an eel's skin, and
even her face and hair were the color of the marsh. Above the
wetland grasses last year's bulrushes waved frowsy heads,
molting brown fuzz in the sunshine. Here and there a black-
bird lit upon a stalk to snatch at the fluff for nest lining,
bending the bulrush and then catapulting back into the sky
as the stem sprang upright. Flæd moved slowly, careful not
to disturb the rising and landing of the birds.

It had taken all her effort to come this far today and find
herself alone. Several days earlier, spring planting had sent
everyone into the fields, including Father John, who was
bound with the members of his order to lend a hand with
plowing and sowing. As soon as they found themselves released from lessons, Flæd and Edward had gone to the woods
together for the first time in many weeks.

That had been an awkward excursion. The brother and

sister had kept to the best-known paths, shying away from trails which were private to the two of them and frequently looking back at the large man who stumped along a little distance behind. They had ended up at the riverbank, sitting glumly on a driftwood branch while Wulf trotted up and down the water's edge.

What can we say to each other, Flæd had fretted. The Mercian crouched a few paces off—close enough to hear any word she uttered. It distressed her that Edward had never yet mentioned her betrothal, but how could she speak plainly of Ethelred, of the wrenching fear she felt each time she thought of leaving her home and family, while her warder was listening? He was Ethelred's man, she knew, and the thought had sealed her lips.

Even after this unsatisfying walk, Flæd had been sure that she and Edward would go to the wood again the next day, but when she asked him, Edward refused to meet her eye.

"It wouldn't be just us," he mumbled. Stung, Flæd glanced toward her warder. "I'm sorry, Flæd," Edward said, pleading now. "It's not the same. I'm going with Father John." Flæd was heartbroken.

In her chamber that night she wondered what else Ethelred of Mercia would take from her before she even left the burgh, before she ever met him. She would not leave for two more seasons, but already her betrothal had pushed her brother away. I will lose nothing more, she thought, staring at her open window as an idea glimmered inside her.

This morning she had walked to the deserted scriptorium alone except for her guardian, who took up his usual position at the entrance. As her warder gazed out into the sunlit street, Flæd stepped back into the shadows. She put one foot on the sill of the window and levered herself up until she could reach the high place where the great poetic codex rested on its side, atop a pile of other books. Quickly, before Red could see, she slung the heavy book under one arm and crouched back at the corner of the open window, whose shutters had been pushed back to let in the warm spring air. She glanced down to find the street empty, as she had hoped, then swiftly maneuvered her body outside and dropped the short distance to the ground.

She began to walk, sliding the book into a leather satchel she had hidden beneath her tunic. Only a few tradespeople were abroad, and Flæd moved as stealthily as she could, slipping around behind the potter's stall, skirting the ovens of baking bread, passing swiftly in front of the open forge where the blacksmith, with his back turned, was beating and folding a bar of glowing metal to make a strong blade. Now only the stone ramparts lay between Flæd and the trees at the edge of the great meadow. Today the masons, spared from field labor, were working inside the unfinished wall. If she could pass unseen through a gap, she would reach the edge of the wood without anyone stopping her.

Picking up two thumbnail-sized pebbles, Flæd crouched down and threw them, hard, at one mason's back. With a yell he spun and swatted at his shirt. The others jeered good-naturedly—no one had thrown anything, they insisted. When he still complained, they went to inspect the welts on their friend's shoulder. As soon as the way was clear, Flæd rounded the wall and ran, her bare feet noiseless on the dusty path, the satchel beating against her legs. Moments later she was concealed in the wood.

The winter lake had receded, leaving a shallow bottom-land covered in downy grass. Beyond the river's opposite bank lay a permanently wet hollow, and for this marsh Flæd was bound. She crossed the silty river, holding the satchel above her shoulders, and then plunged into the marsh. Rushes closed around her, and she began her slow wriggle through the mud.

At the heart of this marsh lay a place Flæd and Edward had discovered in a year of drought. They had wandered along an empty streambed, eventually reaching a gentle rise where a great tree had died. The weight of the dead hulk must have dragged it to earth, where the length of the trunk now lay decaying into the ground. Only the upturned foot of the tree was still whole, though hollowed, with bare, dead roots curling like claws.

Flæd reached the knoll and crept carefully onto the firmer ground. Insects sang in the grasses around her as she wiped mud from her hands and arms and peeled off her sodden outer tunic. She made her way to the fallen tree and settled herself among the roots.

Inside its satchel the book had stayed safe from the damp and muck. Flæd tried to brush the last of the drying mud from her hands before carefully loosening the bindings. She drew out the great codex and placed it gingerly in front of her. I am a thief, Flæd thought, and to her own surprise, she felt no remorse. The half-finished poem had been bothering her. Its characters—the hero, the monster woman, and her son—filled her thoughts. Apparently Alfred had said nothing of her midnight confession to her tutors. No part of the book had appeared among her lesson texts, as she had vainly hoped her father might suggest. Nor, she thought fiercely, could she ever read secretly in the scriptorium again. Mud-spattered, in the middle of a swamp, Flæd opened the book with her first feeling of reckless happiness since becoming the ward of the Mercian envoy.

The hero set off alone in pursuit of the monster woman. She dove beneath the waves of her poisonous pool, and the hero followed, fighting off water serpents, until at last he found her, fought with her, and killed her. Then he beheaded her son, and brought the head to the king to receive the reward he had earned. . . .

With a start Flæd sat up from a dream in which the hero was offering the golden necklace from his treasure hoard to a princess. How had she drowsed off? Looking at the sun, she guessed it was past the ninth hour. She could still return to the burgh well before the workers came home, in plenty of time for prayers. For a moment she worried what her warder might do when she returned. He must be cursing me, Flæd thought to herself, and perversely, the thought made her glad.

Flæd closed her book. She found a dry nook for the satchel deep inside the hollow of the fallen tree, and strapped it tightly to discourage small animals. I will keep it for just a few days more, Flæd decided. I'll try to come back and finish the story. No one will miss the codex tomorrow, or the next day, or even the next, she told herself.

At the foot of the hillock Flæd caught sight of her reflection in the standing water. Her face and hair were grey with dust. The tattered hem of her shift fluttered around her knees, and bits of grass and moss bristled like fur in the dried muck of the tunic she had shrugged on again. For a moment she stared at her image, shocked, and then she threw her arms out with a grin, sending a flock of blackbirds careening up from the mound. I am a monster woman, she thought, a monster woman standing at the edge of her pool.

Flæd followed the stream to the edge of the marsh. She had stayed at the knoll for hours, and had noticed no sign of her warder in the surrounding riverland or woods. Freedom, she thought as she stooped to wash the grit from her arms, had felt sweet even for this little time.

"Lady," a voice behind her said. She whirled to see the Mercian envoy standing half concealed in a stand of young elm trees. "My lady," he said again, stepping forward onto the path, "we should return to the burgh." Flæd stared at him, and then turned wordlessly toward the river. Scuffling ahead of her guardian, she forded the water and crossed through the wood, stepping into the meadow where a stiff wind had begun to blow.

Misery washed over Flæd in waves as the wind dried her clothes. Her time alone had been an illusion, with no true escape from the presence she loathed.

"I should have guessed you were there," she mumbled bitterly into the wind. The steps behind her slowed, and Flæd looked back to see an odd conflict upon her warder's usually impassive face.

"Lady," he said finally, "I was charged to stay with you. Today that duty led me on a weary chase, but I never found the place where you rested all those hours." He snorted, trudging on. "Muddied myself to the waist with trying."

After days of his company, this was the first time Flæd had ever heard her guardian say so much. She could think of no response. She was even more startled to hear the man beside her speak again.

"Your father," he said in a thoughtful tone, "also had success in the marshes." Flæd could make nothing of this.

"What do you mean?" she finally asked.

Red turned to stare at her. "King Alfred's stand at Sumursæte. You haven't heard of it?" Flæd shook her head.

"I thought you were learning history," he muttered. They had reached the wall outside the burgh, where the masons were still at work. "Ask your tutor to show you the Chronicle," he said, stepping aside to let her pass through the gap in the wall. "Find the record of the winters just after your birth. And Lady"—he put out a hand to stop her—"do not go to the marsh without me again. I found these in the wood." In his palm rested two chips of metal. "From a horse's harness," he told her. "The design"—he traced one of the objects with a fingertip—"is not West Saxon."

Flæd was still mulling over this first conversation with her warder when she supped with Edward. She said nothing of her escape to the marsh, or of Red's words—her brother was tired from his day among the furrows, and even Wulf lay spent beneath the table, worn out from chasing birds in the freshly plowed fields. Anyhow, *Edward could have come with me,* she thought wanly as she made her way to the scriptorium. *He probably doesn't care about the poem anymore.*

Father John looked nearly as tired as Edward, but he welcomed her, and nodded politely toward her warder, who had settled by the door. Flæd stood beside John's table in the rushlight.

"Today I heard of an English text"—she hesitated—"a chronicle of my father's reign."

"Yes, the great Chronicle," John replied. "Every burgh in

your father's kingdom has a copy, and with each passing winter their scribes add a report of the year's events."

"I never knew of it before today," Flæd said with some bewilderment. "May I read the Chronicle while you are in the fields?"

"A very good idea," Father John said, smiling. "We have several copies in case of need at other settlements." John crossed the room, took down a recently bound book, and opened it before her. "This one has seen no use since it was written, I think. Pity, for it was long and dull in the copying." Flæd glanced up at him. "I was the scribe," he admitted wryly.

Back in her rooms Flæd lit her own rushlamp and, mounding the bedclothes around her, began to leaf through pages filled with line upon line of Father John's precise script. Sumursæte . . . Sumursæte . . . there! Near the end of the Chronicle she found it, under the entry date 878—five years after her birth, just as her warder had said. The Danes, she read, had routed the West Saxon armies. Alfred and his few remaining men withdrew into the Sumursæte marshes where, in the cold and wet, they hounded the Danish forces. The Danes began to fear this ghostly enemy who struck and vanished and struck again. A spirit of the marsh, some said. A demon, said others. For seven weeks Alfred's tattered and hungry army abused the invaders, and the West Saxon king was never captured.

Flæd closed the book. Pinching out the rushlight, she lay back in her bed. Alfred had kept to his marsh for the course of two moons. Surely, she thought as she burrowed into the feathers, with my warder watching nearby, my marsh will hide me for two more days.

7

Mercia Rallies

THE HERO WAS DYING. HE HAD WON HIS BATTLE AGAINST THE man-monster. He had slain the monster's mother. He had become a king, and had grown old. Now, at last, he stood facing a supreme foe. Flæd sat beside the marsh stump, tears streaking the mud on her face as she held the great book before her.

A dragon raged across the monster slayer's kingdom. Taking the only young retainer who dared to help him, the hero met the worm's horrible strength, braved its fiery breath. The monster broke the hero's sword and seized him in its poisonous jaws. With a dagger the man slashed it open. His young companion stabbed its scorching belly, and together they slew the dragon.

But the hero, now a king, felt the burden of his age and his wounds weighing upon him. He could sense the dragon poison welling into his breast as the young retainer brought armloads of dragon treasure to pile before him.

"I have gained this for my people," the king insisted.

"Now you must serve them." And so the hero died, and over his funeral pyre they raised a great new barrow by the sea.

"And his people said," Flæd read through her tears, "that he was the gentlest and kindest of men, most considerate of his people, and eager to be remembered well."

Flæd closed the book and drew a shuddering sigh. She was sorry for the death of the hero, sorrier still for the end of the story. But the poem's last words were odd, Flæd thought as she returned the book to its hiding place. The final sentence spoke not of the monster killer's battles, but of his gentleness, of his generous care.

Another puzzle, she decided as she slogged to the edge of the marsh. Today Red had walked with her this far and then, by an unspoken agreement, settled back against a tree to wait. Now he came forward, brushing pieces of bark from his bristling hair. He held out a hand to help her onto the path.

"Lady," said the Mercian, "are you hurt?" The fierceness in his tone startled her. Suddenly she remembered the tear streaks on her face.

"It's nothing," Flæd said quickly, scrubbing at her cheeks with a dirty hand. "It was only . . . only a poem I once read. I was thinking about it today." She found herself telling him the story of the hero, of the monsters he had killed, and of the poem's last words, which had seemed so strange to her.

"I heard that poem," Red said slowly, "sung in a great hall for a king who was a warrior like your monster killer—

he had fought his enemies for many years. But in the end"—
the Mercian had begun to toy with the heavy band of metal
on his wrist—"that king deserted his people." Red said nothing for such a long time that Flæd began to think their conversation had ended. Then he spoke again. "If war struck this
place, would your father leave your sisters, your youngest
brother, or Edward in danger?"

Flæd shook her head, upset by the suggestion. "He would
die first, and so would I," she said with heat.

"A king must take care of his people as well as your father
takes care of his children," Red said, "the way we all try to
protect our families—even," he added, almost in a whisper,
"when we can't."

That night, as Flæd and Edward sat together in a dark
corner of the kitchen, she decided to explain at last how she
had taken the great codex. "You read it without me, Flæd?"
he cried, forgetting to speak softly in his disappointment.
Because you refused to come with me, Flæd remembered,
but she spoke gently to her brother, soothing him.

"There are many other poems in the book," she whispered, "stories of saints and strange beasts and other heroes.
Tomorrow I'll bring it back, and you and I will find another
time to read it." A little sulky, Edward agreed. "Shall I tell
you the rest of the story?" Flæd said, poking his rib.

"All right." Edward squirmed, batting at her hand. So she
told him, and Edward's eyes widened in the dim light.

"A dragon," he echoed when she described the last monster. "I'd like to find a dragon's barrow, and kill the dragon, and take the gold."

"Then what would you do?" Flæd asked, skeptically.

"I would build a great hall, and cover the roof and the walls with gold, and hang golden horns above the door, and I would sit on a high seat decorated with twisted gold, and drink from a golden cup."

"Very fine," Flæd said with a smile. "And what about the dragon?"

"What about it?"

"The dragon's body. What would you do with the stinking thing?"

"Wulf and I would drag it into the sea," Edward decided. "Or into the river," he added, "if we found one to kill around here."

Flæd nodded seriously. She finished the story for her brother, reciting the poem's last lines of praise for the king. Edward listened, and then added his own resolution.

"In my golden hall we will also give out treasure to everyone in the kingdom," he said with satisfaction.

"We?" Flæd asked.

"Wulf and I," Edward said, and Flæd laughed for the first time since Red had come.

Back in her own quarters Flæd rolled her ruined shift and tunic into a tight ball and squeezed them into the space beside her bed, next to the wad of yesterday's clothes. The serving women, she felt sure, would not be happy to find these little bundles, but she wanted the clothes to stay hidden until tomorrow at least, when she hoped to return the book safely to its shelf. Not everyone would accommodate her strange project as her warder had done, Flæd suspected, and it would be better if the serving women knew nothing until it was finished. In her sleeping shift she brushed her hair and braided it again. As she bound the end of the plait, she heard low voices outside her door, and then a soft tap on the door frame.

"Lady," came Red's voice through the cloth hanging, "the bishop wants a word with you."

Asser? Flæd had not seen her former tutor for several weeks. She threw a woolen blanket around her shoulders and came to the door.

"My lady Æthelflæd," Bishop Asser said with a nod, "I am sorry if I have disturbed you. Today your father told me that from now on your lessons should include readings from the great poetic codex in our scriptorium. He apologizes for neglecting to mention this to your tutors sooner. And I apologize," the Bishop added, "for underestimating your talents. I should never be too busy to recognize a gifted scholar."

"I—I thank you," stammered Flæd. "I . . . I know the great book."

"I have asked Father John to bring it to your table in the morning."

"Tomorrow?" Flæd asked in a panic.

"Yes, the planting is nearly done, and Father John can be spared from the fields. I am sorry," he finished with a ghost of a smile, "that your holiday has ended so soon. Sleep well, Lady Æthelflæd."

Asser walked on, and Flæd stood stricken by the doorway.

"Lady, what troubles you?" Red asked softly.

"I . . . I am weary from our long day," she replied miserably. "Good night."

Flæd went back into the darkness of her room and slumped onto her bed. She looked up at her shuttered window. No, she could not escape that way. Her warder would be ready if she tried such a thing again. And she was sure he would not allow a midnight trip to the marsh. Tomorrow would bring shame, and perhaps punishment. She would have to tell them, and bear the consequences.

Flæd slept fitfully that night, and dreamt of her father on his high seat, eyeing her with disappointment. On either side of him the carved dragons spat out their tails and hissed in her direction, their ruby eyes balefully agleam. "Thiefffff," the dragons whispered to her father. "Thiefffff . . ."

In the morning she had no stomach for breakfast. She dressed slowly and sat in her room until it was time to leave for the scriptorium. Reluctantly she crossed the burgh and entered the stone building, eyes on the floor as she walked toward the table where Father John and Edward waited.

"Lady," Father John called out, and she looked up guiltily. Then she stared. The great codex lay open on the table. "A special text today," Father John was saying. "Edward tells me you both know the story of the monster slayer. I thought we might start instead with some riddles." Flæd stood motionless for another long moment, then forced herself to walk the remaining distance to the table. She seated herself on the bench beside them with a thump, eyes still fixed on the book. She put out a hand to touch the thing. Yes, this was certainly the same beautiful vellum of the volume she had hidden in the marsh, the same elegant script.

"I am glad your father suggested this collection for our lessons," John was saying. "The book seems rather dusty from staying too long on its shelf." He leaned forward to brush his hand across the page. Edward looked at Flæd, quirking his dark eyebrows into a question. Flæd could only shrug her shoulders in return.

That morning they read riddles, and Flæd tried to concentrate on the short, twisting poems, working out their solutions. "Wind" was the answer to one, "Shield" to another, and "Cock and Hen" was the answer to a brief and bawdy poem whose scrambled rune letters spelled out the names of the two creatures.

By the time of the midday meal Flæd suspected that she had found a solution to another of the day's mysteries. Leaving Edward and John at their table, she carried dark bread and cheese to the corner where her warder sat. The man looked haggard, accepting the food with a nod, and beginning to eat hungrily as she sat down beside him.

"You knew about the book?" she asked him abruptly.

For a moment he stopped eating, and then said simply, "I guessed."

"You found the fallen tree in the marsh?"

"I watched from the top of a tree yesterday. You weren't as careful. One of your father's guards sat at your door last night instead of me." He waited for a moment in silence, and then began tearing at the bread again. A slow grin spread across Flæd's face.

"You had no sleep, and no breakfast?" she asked.

"None," he agreed, returning her smile.

8

A Mound on the Plain

WITH A CRY OF FRUSTRATION FLÆD FELT THE NIB OF HER QUILL give way and watched another blot spread across her scrap of vellum. Her little piece of parchment had begun to look like the skin of a blighted fruit. Glumly she gazed at the feather pen's frayed point.

"Four pens ruined in a day," Father John intoned, appearing at her shoulder. He shook his head. "Surely, my lady, you can do better than that." He glanced sideways at her as her shoulders slumped forward, then continued, "I ruined seven on my first day."

Catlike, John sidestepped the quill his pupil tried to fling in his direction as she attempted not to smile. He seated himself smoothly beside Edward at the other end of the bench. "You will have noticed," he lectured, "the many differences between quill and stylus. By this latest experiment you have revealed another: A feather is an even less effective missile than a stick."

Sighing, Flæd turned back to the irregular page of writing in front of her. The parchment had never been a thing of beauty. Holes and scars marked the surface of the thin animal hide, which had been cured not to white perfection, but to the hue of tallow. The edge of the sheepskin had spoiled the squaring of the page, so instead of four corners the page showed just three, and one ragged diagonal side. Father John had deposited a handful of quills by her place at the table that morning. With small, sharp knives the two of them had shaped the quill points, and then he had left her alone with ink and a passage of religious history to copy.

It was past the eighth hour, and Flæd bit her lip with concentration as she leaned over her work. She dipped the last of her prepared quills gingerly into the ink. Three characters later Flæd stopped, watching the ink of an *s*'s long tail bleed into the *m* and the *o* which had preceded it.

"For a moment I felt certain that blot spelled *mos,*" Father John announced, looking over her shoulder again. "Yes, *Mos,* the Latin word meaning 'custom.' Surely the custom of our own classroom would permit an early finish to a day filled with such, er, diligent application of the pen. Read a passage of the Chronicle before you come tomorrow."

With relief Flæd cleared away her things and left the scriptorium along with Edward and Wulf. The three of them trudged through the dusty street toward their quarters, with Wulf frisking back once to touch his nose to the hand of the warder, who walked behind them.

"Come fishing with us, Flæd," Edward said. Flæd almost

stopped walking in surprise. Edward had not invited her to join him for a ramble in weeks—ever since the grim little walk they had taken to the riverbank. She had tried to resign herself to their new relationship—together in the classroom, conversations at meals, but no real time to themselves.

"You know I can't come alone," she said, lowering her voice.

Edward glanced back at Red. "I forget about him now, most of the time," he said softly to her. "It doesn't matter if he's with us. Come to the river." Flæd felt a lump rising in her throat. This is the best we can do, Edward seemed to be saying. But it was good—it was better than simply missing him each afternoon. Flæd pretended to brush a fly from her face, hoping her brother would not see her emotion. I'd better do the reading Father John wants first, she told herself. We might stay awhile at the river.

"You go ahead and see if the fish are hungry," Flæd told him, stopping between their father's council chamber and the family's buildings. "I'll do Father John's lesson as fast as I can, and then I'll meet you." Edward made a good-natured face at his sister. He would have rushed through such studying at breakfast, his look seemed to say. Flæd gave him a mock scowl in return, and ducked into her quarters. Grabbing her volume of the Chronicle, she found the passage where she had left off and started to read. But she could hardly concentrate on the words. Edward is waiting for me— the thought circled cheerfully in her mind like Wulf chasing his tail. With a sigh of impatience, she closed the book, tucked it under her arm, and hurried out toward the meadow.

At the burgh wall Flæd seated herself in the sun where it glowed upon the sandy stone blocks. In the distance she could see two small figures, Edward and Wulf, making their way along the riverbank toward the place where they planned to fish. The tiny Edward raised his arm to point at something ahead of them, and the tiny Wulf loped forward, veering out into the meadow.

A little sound made Flæd turn her head, and she saw her warder crouching down against the wall a short way off. Flæd's spirits dimmed. It was easy for Edward to say he didn't care about the Mercian envoy's company. Despite her guardian's favors, Flæd felt more and more restless as the days of protection continued with no sign of any danger.

It was worse when she tried to understand what she was waiting for. Ethelred remained a faceless name to her, Mercia was an outline on a map, and Lunden was a dot inside it. She had watched her mother these past weeks, trying to imagine how she must have felt when she came from Mercia to marry Alfred. Ealhswith and Alfred must have thought their daughter would learn to accept her betrothal, the way they had settled into their lives with each other. Well, Flæd thought with a quiver of fear and stubbornness, I haven't.

Think about something else, Flæd told herself, ducking her head unhappily and opening her book. She had been reading about the constant threat of Danish settlers, who

seized English land for themselves and their families. Today
Flæd read the entry for the year 871. Alfred and his brother
met the enemy at Readingas. The Danes had occupied an
earthwork—a great mounded wall of earth fronted by a
broad trench deeper than a man was tall—to protect themselves in the flat land between two rivers. Nine times Alfred
and his brother rode to battle that season, the Chronicle
stated. Nine times they faced the Danes in their earthwork
defenses, and gained only a single victory.

Flæd thought of her father, only a few years beyond his
twentieth winter, riding exhausted into skirmish after skirmish. Secure behind their earthwork, the Danes held fast,
and Alfred's brother died before the winter came again.
Young and battle-weary, Alfred became the king of the battered West Saxon kingdom. "And in that year," the Chronicle's entry finished bleakly, "were slain nine earls and one
king."

Flæd closed the book. Father John would be satisfied with
this much reading—she had done her duty. She looked out
over the meadow again. She could no longer see Wulf and
Edward, but now she wanted very much to be with them, to
sit with them on the grassy riverbank watching for the quick
brown and silver fish. Hefting herself to her feet, she set out
across the meadow with her book.

In the center of the broad pasture Flæd could see a little
band of horses, their heads lowered to the tender spring
grass. As she drew closer she could hear the sound of their

blunt teeth tearing at the short blades. Flæd knew many of these horses. Some belonged to the retainers who lived in this burgh with the royal family, and others were owned by the royal family itself. Flæd approached the little group. The horse nearest to her raised its head to watch her coming. Then it turned and with the other horses began moving away. Flæd stopped, and the horses started to graze again, eyeing her.

What was bothering them? In the center of the herd a dun horse looked up and snorted at something behind her. She glanced back. Red stood a little distance away, unable to blend into a shadow or fade back against a wall in this wide open pasture. Flæd groaned. What could possibly endanger her out here? Trying to conceal her impatience, she walked back to him.

"The horses don't know you," Flæd told her warder. "They're nervous. Will you wait here? I'll just go to the horses, and then come back." Red looked around them for a long moment. No other human figures were visible in the vast open stretch of land. Then he nodded.

"I will keep the book for you, Lady," he offered. He was right—she ought not to risk the valuable thing among the animals. Flæd handed him the volume, then turned to approach the horses once again. This time they gathered around her, whickering softly and brushing her arms and hands with whiskery mouths. She patted their shaggy sides, and a few long winter hairs floated away. "Jewel-bright," she said softly, remembering the name of the mare with the white star between her eyes. She scratched the fuzzy hollow between the mare's jawbones. "Gold-friend," she greeted the big dun gelding, leader of the little herd, who bumped her shoulder with his nose when she turned aside to smooth another horse's mane.

When the horses were sure she had brought nothing for them to eat, they returned to their forage. She looked around her and thought she understood why they had chosen this little rise for their grazing site. From this high place every inch of the pasture was visible. Flæd was surprised to find a slight bowl worn into the surface of the earth at the peak of the hill. The ground was very dry, almost sandy. The horses have used this place as a wallow, she thought to herself, hallowing it out as they roll in the dust. As if to prove her point, a sorrel yearling knelt down and began to roll, kicking his legs in ridiculous pleasure as he eased the itch of his first winter coat.

Descending from the mound she looked back. No sign of the depression at its crest was visible from the pasture below. It hides the horses' clumsy baths, she thought to herself.

Flæd's spirits sank as she returned to her warder. Duty brings me back, she sighed, as surely as duty kept my father on the plain at Readingas where the Danish earthwork defeated him so many times. No wonder her father had begun to use fortifications himself after such a crushing blow. She imagined the Danish horde, massed safely behind their protective wall. They would have been able to look down on the West Saxon armies and watch them come from a great distance off. Danish sentries lying flat at the top of the fortification must have been nearly invisible. . . .

All at once Flæd was no longer thinking of her father. Earthwork. A place from which to see, but not be seen. Her mind tumbled over the beginnings of an idea that had just come to her. She would need to ask Father John more about that passage in the Chronicle she had read. She would need some way to cross an open space undetected. And here was the most difficult thing: Absolutely no one must suspect her until the moment she carried out her plan.

"Three already, Flæd!" The girl jumped at the voice. Caught up in her thoughts, she had hardly noticed as she and Red approached the riverbank where Edward sprawled in the afternoon sun. Now the boy held up a stick with three fish strung along it through the gills, one almost the length of his forearm. "And look." He pointed to the tangle of bushes on the opposite bank. Flæd saw a flash of green and blue plummet from a branch overhanging the water. Only a ripple, quickly swallowed by the eddying water, showed where the strike had happened, and back on its branch a bright, crested bird raised its beak to swallow the small fish it had captured.

"Kingfisher." Flæd grinned at her brother. It was a sign of

luck to see the little bird. As she seated herself beside Edward, she stole a glance at her warder, who had found his own seat beside a knob of rock upon which he had balanced her copy of the Chronicle. It would take all the luck she could muster, Flæd knew, to make another escape from Red.

9

Mercia Bested

"YOU WANT TO KNOW MORE ABOUT EARTHWORK DEFENSES."
Father John tapped the open page of Flæd's Chronicle
thoughtfully. "I am not a fighting man, but I have spoken to
some who went against the Danes at Readingas. I can tell
you what I learned." Flæd folded her hands and tried to adopt
a look of simple curiosity. She had come to her lessons with
this question prepared, but her tutor must not guess that
she had a special reason for asking. The young priest went
on.

"You understand that 'earthwork' means a protection
built by digging up the ground and piling it high on one side
of the pit left by the digging." Flæd nodded. "The defenders
then have a wall overlooking a trench. They can watch their
enemies approaching—on a plain such as the one at Readingas, the Danes could see the West Saxon armies coming long
before they were close enough to begin combat. When the
attackers reach the earthwork, they are slowed by the trench
and often halted by the wall. The defenders then have an-

other advantage of height: Their blows and missiles come down upon the enemy, while the attackers must climb and strike upward. Even a smaller force can win a battle with the help of an earthwork defense."

"The earthwork at Readingas, it was on a plain, by a river?"

"On a plain between two rivers," Father John corrected her. "The thanes I asked about the battle told me that on some mornings the Danes remained entirely concealed as your father and his brother led their army into the place of battle. An empty rise was all the West Saxons saw, until the Danes chose to show themselves." Just as I imagined, thought Flæd, feeling a further spark of excitement which she was careful not to reveal to her tutor.

"Of course, there are other earthworks in your father's holdings, and in the Danelaw," the priest continued. "Some dykes the men of Rome built when they conquered these lands long before any Saxons made their home here. Many hundreds of years ago a great king of the Mercians also made a vast earthwork between his own kingdom and the territory of the Welsh princes to the west. When he can, your father tries to use these ancient defenses to strengthen his own borders. And he has a new interest, I understand, in another sort of earthwork. . . ."

"Another sort?" Flæd repeated, cocking her head.

"Yes," John answered, drawing a wax tablet and stylus toward him. "A kind of fortress designed—I think this is the best way to describe it—like an earthwork wall, only built in a ring." As the priest spoke, he began to sketch. "The earth from the encircling trench would be piled in the center, here, until the workers had made a hill, a hill which appeared flat at the summit. In fact that even-looking crest was the wall around the rim of a fortress, within which were shelters for people and animals. In times of war folk who farmed the land around such a fortress could bring their families and their beasts into the high fortress for safety. I believe your father has found and occupied several of these places, and is strengthening them for his own army's defense."

Flæd looked at the flat-topped hill her tutor had drawn in the wax. My face will betray me now, she thought with a flush. But how could she ignore the way Father John's picture suggested the natural shape of a hill which figured in her own plans?

Late that afternoon Flæd stood again at the edge of the meadow. She took a few steps out into the open space and raised two fingers to her mouth, making the loud whistle she had seen some townsfolk use to call their animals. For a moment she waited anxiously, looking out into the pasture. Then she saw the little herd of horses coming at a trot. Flæd was ready for them this time, carrying a leather pouch filled with oatcakes she had taken from the kitchen that morning, and a handful of wrinkled brown apples from a basket she had found among the burgh's winter stores. She fed the horses bits of oatcake and apple, talking to them and stroking them, until her pouch was nearly empty. The horses began to drift away into the pasture one by one, until only two were left standing beside her, eyeing the pouch as she dangled it by the strings.

"So you are the greediest pair," she scolded, scratching the nearest one beneath his forelock as he nudged at the pouch. In fact they were a matched pair, Flæd could see, dappled grey with lighter grey manes and tails. Their hooves were pale, veined with tiny black streaks, and both had a white stocking on the off hind foot. Flæd remembered these two horses now, twin foals born three winters ago and put to harness just last autumn. She felt sure that both had also felt the weight of a rider during their training.

"Oat," she named the one who snorted at the last pippin she offered him, but nibbled the cake delicately from her hand. "Apple," she called his brother, who happily took the fruit and stood swishing his tail as she hung the empty pouch around her neck. These horses were taller and heavier than the pony she and Edward used to share, but Flæd twisted her fingers in Oat's mane, kilted up her tunic, and took the two running steps she had learned to use when mounting from the ground. As she threw her leg across the horse's broad back, Oat heaved his sides in a sigh and looked around at her. He lowered his head to the grass, as if protesting the end of his long winter of liberty. But Flæd clucked to bring his head up and pressed her knees together, sending him forward.

She rode Oat along the wall, with Apple tagging curiously beside them. They turned back in the direction from which they had started, and Flæd saw that Red had stepped forward. She nodded to him as she passed with the two horses, and he folded his arms across his chest. Flæd rode Oat in a circle, then made a looping figure, changing his direction by shifting her weight to one side, then the other. Finally she brought him to a stand by settling back and softly giving the command a driver uses to halt a team. She patted the horse's neck and glanced sideways at the Mercian. He ran his fingers through his short brush of hair with an unreadable expression on his hard face. Then he went back to his seat beside the wall.

The next afternoon Flæd called the herd again, but this time fed only the matched pair. She rode Apple, and found his trot a little harder, and his canter a little longer than Oat's. But both horses had the same willing response to her weight upon their backs and her quiet words, even without saddle or bridle. "You have sold your freedom," she lectured them after the ride, "for a bit of sweet food and a scratch behind the ear." With a slap on Apple's rump, she sent them off.

Flæd came to the pasture every day after her lessons, and every day she rode a little further into the meadow. She found she could ride either horse in a variety of positions: crouched on the withers, stretched out along its back, or even with her arms clasped awkwardly around the horse's neck, as long as she continued to urge it forward. The horses took no notice of any amount of mane-pulling, she had discovered as she wrapped her hands in the long hair to steady herself at a gallop, or to ease herself to the ground when their ride had finished. Oat and Apple were tall, and she would have to hang briefly, suspending almost her whole weight from the mane as she brought her right leg over the horse's back and then dropped two-footed onto the ground.

She hesitated for a moment as she was dismounting one afternoon, hanging from the mane and keeping one toe hooked across Oat's back. A person on the other side of the horse, where Red is sitting, could hardly see me, she thought to herself, and slipped a little lower, thinking about this odd position. Impatient, Oat took a few steps forward, and Flæd swung wildly for a second, bringing her other foot up to hook the back of her left big toe around the bones at the base of Oat's neck. Now I am truly a foolish sight, Flæd thought in some confusion as she hung almost upside down on one side of her horse. Why didn't I dismount? Then she had a thought which made her lower her feet and drop to the ground very quickly in the hope that Red had not seen her hanging there, and not because she feared his opinion of her foolishness. If her idea worked, she had found a way around the final obstacle to her scheme.

The next day Flæd rode Oat out far enough that she could barely see her warder in his place against the yellow wall. She walked her horse with his near side—the side on which he had been trained to let a rider mount—toward the river, and his other side toward the burgh. Softly she repeated the command to go forward and slipped halfway down on the left side, as if dismounting. Oat balked, but at her insistence kept walking, and Flæd brought her other foot up to his withers as she had the day before. This was awkward, but not impossible, not even very difficult, she thought as she swung along, her braid brushing the grass beside Oat's feet. She clucked to him, urging him into a trot, but at the first jounces of the new gait she felt her fingers slipping in the mane, and with a grunt she fell, rolling to keep away from the horse's hooves. She lay there looking up at the sky, breathing hard and feeling slightly bruised as Oat came back and lowered his nose to the familiar pouch on its string around her neck. He nibbled at the leather. Apple, always close behind, joined them, staring at the prostrate human. At least Red didn't see, Flæd thought.

Through the remainder of the week Flæd experimented with the strange new riding stance, and found that if she wove a knot into the horse's mane she could slip to the side during a canter or a gallop, and even pull herself back up again without the difficulty the jarring trot gave her. Far from the wall she practiced, first tucking the end of her braid between her teeth and urging her mount into a gallop, and then slipping down to cling to the horse's flank. Afterward she would trot with her dappled pair back to the burgh wall, where Red was always waiting. Dismounting with a last word of praise for the greys, she would go back through the narrowing gap in the wall, Red close behind her, and pass through the streets on her way to evensong and supper.

On one such night she met Asser and her father. "Æthelflæd," the king smiled as he caught sight of her, "you have been in the wind on the meadow, I see. Your head is as shaggy as the horses' winter coats." Flæd tucked the strands of hair behind her ears.

"Their coats are almost smooth now," she told him.

"I see," Alfred said, turning her around, "that you have decided to wear their winter dress for them." Her clothes were covered with long grey hairs. "We will not send these clothes with you to Mercia," Alfred said thoughtfully. "Ethelred will hardly expect his bride to arrive in a hair shirt."

Flæd could not reply—the joke reminded her painfully of a journey she refused to contemplate. She brushed at her tunic, and felt her father's light hand upon her head for a moment before he and Asser continued on.

"My lady," Asser said as he passed, "how go your lessons? Have you learned some new skill since last we spoke?"

Flæd considered several answers she could give to such a question. "My writing on parchment is much improved," she said with a solemn nod.

That night Flæd stared at the moon through the open window above her bed. She had believed that she had surmounted every challenge in the way of her plan, but tonight she had to face one last quandary. A part of her felt sure that carrying out her scheme would betray her unspoken agreement with Red, as well as her understanding with her father. They trust me, she thought. Then she remembered Red's compromise at the marsh: He had let her go in again, without knowing exactly where she would hide herself. Is my plan for tomorrow so different, Flæd wondered. She turned the dilemma over in her mind until the half-circle of moon climbed higher into the sky, and she slept.

Flæd stood at the edge of the meadow and raised ink-stained fingers to her mouth to whistle for the horses. My writing *has* improved, she thought, inspecting the black marks on her skin. Now I blot my hands more than the page. Apple and Oat trotted up alone—the other horses stayed nose-deep in the sweet grass.

Flæd mounted Apple and cantered out into the meadow with Oat close behind them. She passed the limit of her previous rides and rode further still. Looking back, she thought she could see Red leave the wall and come toward her at a quick walk. She would have to act now, or not at all.

Flæd urged her mount into a gallop, riding crouched at the withers. Her guardian would not be able to reach her on foot, she confirmed with another backward glance at his struggling shape. At her bidding, the two grey horses veered around and headed toward the little knoll where the herd had gathered as usual. With her mount's other side toward her warder, Flæd slipped down on the near side as she had practiced, urging Apple forward until he had crested the hill, which slowed him to a canter. All at once Flæd released her hold on Apple's mane and dropped into the dusty hollow. She rolled away, speaking one final command, which sent the pair a little further on before they slowed to a trot and turned back to join the grazing herd. Flæd crept to the edge of the little bowl and lay still while her breathing quieted, listening.

She heard Red's footsteps when he reached the foot of the hillock, heard him talking softly to the horses as he moved among them and found the greys, but not their rider. Chin pressed to the ground, she peered through the short grass and saw Red stroking Apple's wet neck, and swinging up onto his back. Her warder looked right and left, searching the flat land for some sign of his charge. Then he turned the horse toward a cluster of trees beside the river, the only cover nearby. As he rounded the foot of the rise Flæd could hear him speaking under his breath, "Stupid slave. Still a stupid slave."

Apple's hoofbeats faded, but Flæd kept watching until Red, Apple, and Oat, who tagged along after them, had disappeared among the branches of the distant trees. When she was sure they had gone for good, Flæd rolled onto her back to look at the soft clouds that had covered the afternoon sky. She considered what she had done. She had strained the limits of duty. She had used her family's horses and her father's battlefield history to deceive a man devoted to her protection. Flæd knew these things, but at this moment, alone and unwatched by any other person, she closed her eyes and felt satisfied.

What were the strange words Red had said? *Still a stupid slave.* Flæd had not understood this, and now she decided that she didn't care. She listened to the horses as they moved about the little hill, hearing their soft breath and the swish of their tails. One trotted past the edge of the hollow where she lay, and she opened her eyes as the hoofbeats thumped up. The colt was rolling its eye so that the white showed. Silly thing, she thought, arching her neck to see it go. Several other horses nearby tossed their heads and followed.

"Don't be nervous," she murmured. "You know me, remember? This is our safe place, our own earthwork."

She never saw the heavy sack as it descended over her head. She heard her own strangled screams as the cloth was pressed firmly against her face. She struggled weakly against the deft hands that bound her arms, her ankles. Someone was wadding the sacking into her mouth and pushing up her lower jaw so that almost no sound could escape her heavily muffled mouth. Soon it was all she could do to keep from suffocating. A thong bound the gag in place. Her shoulders were lifted, then her ankles. At least two of them, she registered through her panic, taking me away . . . *where is Red?*

10

Treachery

THE WOOLEN SACK RASPED AGAINST FLÆD'S CHEEK AS IT WAS
jerked away from her face. Cool forest air poured over her as
she lay on the ground. She flailed onto her side and tried to
scream again, but a powerful hand clamped across her
mouth. Her chin was wrenched up and the point of a blade
touched the hollow of her throat.

"No. Do not call." The words were spoken in strangely ac-
cented English. Flæd grew still, and after a moment the hand
was removed, although the dagger remained. The jolting run
from the pasture had seemed to take forever as her captors
roughly bundled her along with them, but now she guessed
that not much time had passed—the sun coming through
the trees still stood high in the afternoon sky. She lay
stretched out on the ground in a thicket. The man who had
spoken was no longer looking down at her, although his dagger never left her neck. His head was cocked, as if he listened
for some sound. Two other men crouched nearby, looking
out toward the meadow and speaking quietly to each other

in a language Flæd didn't understand. They were strongly
built, and Flæd could see that they were dressed in a light,
leather armor like the kind her warder wore. These men were
prepared for combat.

One of them addressed the person holding the knife, who
then turned his dark, bearded face back to Flæd.

"You walk. Hide us from the thane." He gestured to include all four of them, then stared at Flæd until she nodded.
These men have been watching me, she realized with a fresh
burst of horror. They have learned that I know these woods
better than they do, and better than the "thane"—my
warder. Holding his dagger between his teeth, her captor
began loosening the bonds at her ankles until she could take
hobbled steps. The three men took up positions around her,
and with the knife against her spine, they set off.

Flæd stumbled forward, her mind teeming with ways
these men might intend to hurt her. My fault, my fault, a
voice inside of her repeated. My fault for leaving Red. How
will he find me? How will anyone find me? Tears of shame
and terror blinded her as she tramped on, goaded by a rough
hand on her elbow, the prick of the knife on her back. Grad-
ually her jolting steps focused her attention back on the path.
She saw a familiar group of rocks, then a tree she knew. A
memory rose up among her crippled thoughts. Red walking
back with her from the marsh. "Would your father leave
your sisters, your youngest brother, or Edward in danger? . . .
A king must take care of his people as well as your father

takes care of his children, the way we all try to protect our families." Red would fight to protect anyone entrusted to his care. He will not stop looking, Flæd suddenly felt sure. Trying to ignore the scrape of the blade against her clothes, she began to make a plan.

Shuffling forward as if she were reluctant to choose this route, Flæd led the men across the river at a place close to the ford she and Red had used earlier that spring. As they entered the marsh where Flæd had hidden the great codex, the men exchanged words again, and Flæd thought she heard approval in their voices. I think they saw me lose Red here, she shivered. They must have been watching us all that time.

When they reached the fallen tree, Flæd was made to sit among the roots. Her feet were lashed tightly together again, her wrists bound to the gnarled wood. They are waiting for something, she realized as her limbs began to grow numb.

They are waiting for darkness, she understood at last, wrists and ankles throbbing with her heartbeat as the long minutes stretched into hours, and the sun sank lower and lower into the west. One abductor had settled down in front of her while the other two took turns keeping watch at the edges of the knoll. I was wrong to think of coming here, after all, she thought hopelessly. Red has not remembered.

The man who had spoken to her in English wandered up to the giant log, his eyes fixed on Flæd. In the language the three men shared, he said something to Flæd's guard—a question, Flæd thought. The other man responded with an ugly smile, and Flæd jerked in fright as he stood, and the two of them approached her.

With a rush of wings, a flock of birds took flight on the outskirts of the marsh. Flæd's captors crouched down, and the man standing at the edge of the hillock hissed out to the other two, who went to join him, running low. They huddled at the little vantage point, and Flæd wondered in vain what they could see. A jolt of hope had surged through her when the birds rose, and as soon as she was left alone, she had begun to strain futilely and painfully at the leather thongs they had used to tie her. Would a big man like her warder be able to creep secretly through the marsh as she had, even with three pairs of hostile eyes watching for him?

"Be silent," a familiar voice murmured in her ear. One by one Flæd felt her bonds strain and give way to a blade. "Get behind me." She was shoved back into the hollow as Red finished freeing her and rushed out.

Flæd could barely feel her arms and legs. She tried to get up and flopped onto her belly, her face pressing into the decayed wood underfoot. Whimpering and trying to rub life back into her limbs, Flæd heard the sounds of the struggle outside—grunts punctuated by harsh words in the foreign tongue of the three enemies, the scuffling of feet in the grass, bodies falling, a gurgling scream and more running steps, then silence.

Three of them, and he was all alone, she thought frantically as she fought to make her limbs support her. They will come for me next! She scrabbled in the rotting wood for something to use as a weapon. There was a rock she could lift just outside the stump, she thought she remembered. Crawling on hands and knees afire with pain, Flæd inched forward into the clearing.

Red was kneeling a short distance away from her, breathing heavily. Beside him lay one of the men who had taken Flæd. Flæd's mouth was still dry with fear. She found she still could not stand up, so she kept crawling toward her guardian.

"Lady." Red got to his feet and came to her. "Are you injured?" He touched the welts the bonds had left on her arms.

"Where are the others?" she croaked hoarsely. "There were three. . . ."

"Two ran. One of them was the leader, I think." Red helped her to her feet and brought her to the form lying in the grass. Still catching his breath, he crouched down and rolled the man over. It was not the one who had spoken English to her, who seemed to be the leader, as Red had rightly guessed. Flæd could not remember which of the others this had been. He was clearly dead. "When he went down," Red was saying, "the two others disappeared." Flæd was shaking. She had seen the blood of slaughtered animals, but this was different.

"What happened in the pasture?" she heard her warder ask. Flæd could not stop staring at the man on the ground. This person had bound and threatened her—for this she would have wished him punished, hurt, and shamed. But the man lay dead. She had believed her warder would protect her. She had not considered the fact that he would kill for her. Flæd was still foolishly clutching the rock she had crawled outside to find, and now she dropped it. Her warder had asked her a question. How could she ever explain what had happened?

"I—I fell from the horse," she rasped, putting her hand to her parched throat. "They surprised me." Flæd turned away so that she wouldn't have to look at her warder, or the body beside him. *A man is dead because of me.* She couldn't tell Red what she had done.

"I thought you ran away." Red shook his head, rummaging in the litter of the camp to find a waterskin, which he brought to Flæd. "She might go to the marsh again, I told myself. So I came here. When I heard them coming, I hid. I wanted to free you sooner, Lady," he said, sounding angry at himself as he held out a hand to steady her as she drank.

"I hoped you would remember this place," Flæd mumbled guiltily. "Something frightened the birds—I thought it might be you."

"No. Your horses," Red said. "I left them by the stream." His hands were busy now searching the dead man's clothes. He pried the dagger from the man's hand and gave it to Flæd. "We need to go," he told her. "The others may come back."

Red would not let Flæd ride alone. He mounted Apple

and pulled her up behind him. At the burgh wall they sent the greys back to the herd, and Flæd stood with her head down, knowing more surely than ever that she should tell her warder what had really happened. But still she could not make her tongue say the words, and Red spoke instead.

"Lady, I must see the king. I ask you to come with me." His voice was hard and empty, and above the dull metal around his neck, his face was grim. Humbly Flæd nodded, and at Red's gesture preceded him along the street toward her father's chambers.

They found him there with Asser and Father John. The three of them looked up from a manuscript when Flæd and the Mercian warder entered, and all stood as Alfred greeted the envoy.

"Welcome, thane of Ethelred. The light is fading, and still we abuse our eyes with this Latin script at the end of a long day. You have spared me a difficult passage of translation which my bishop and mass priest are too polite to finish for me," he said with a tired smile. "Please, tell us how we may be of use to you."

"I have been of little enough use to you," Red said in a low voice. "King Alfred, I must surrender my duties. I do not deserve the trust you have placed in me to protect the lady Æthelflæd." Flæd drew a sharp breath. Somehow she had expected a rebuke, not this. Alfred and his advisors exchanged looks of confusion.

"Surely you have kept her safe—she is here with us now,

well and carefully guarded. What trust have you broken?" Alfred wondered.

"I have not kept my vow," Red insisted. "Today she was stolen from my care." Tersely he described Flæd's disappearance, and the fight in the marsh. He showed them the marks on her wrists and ankles, and the tiny cut where the dagger had pressed against her throat. "I should never have lost sight of her," he declared, his voice heavy with self-condemnation. "I ask that you release me from your service and let me go back to Mercia. Your own thanes will serve you more honorably than I have." Red looked around him, suddenly uncertain what to say next. "I will wait at the lady's quarters," he said slowly. "I will keep watch this last night."

Alfred gazed at the man for a long moment, then nodded. "Go then, and in the morning we will make a better farewell." He watched the envoy turn and disappear through the doorway. "But I would know more of this matter," the king said under his breath. He looked at Flæd, who stood motionless where her warder had left her. "What happened, child?" Alfred asked.

11

Truce

FLÆD SAW LINES OF WORRY AROUND HER FATHER'S EYES. "HE did not fail you," she said, and stumbled with shame over her next words. "I—I . . . led him to believe that he did." Wretchedly she told the story again, including her guilty part in it. The light in the room was nearly gone, and for a long time the four people who stood together in the dusk said nothing. At last Flæd spoke again. "I will ask him to stay," she whispered miserably. "I will ask pardon of our Mercian guest."

Alfred sat down again with a sigh. Father John began lighting the candles at the corners of the table.

"John, Asser," her father said, and the young priest halted his task. "Our reading seems somewhat heavy tonight. Perhaps the writings of Pope Gregory would be better."

"We will bring the *Dialogues*," Asser said with a bow, and he and John left the room.

"Æthelflæd," her father said when they were alone, "you have been unhappy these past weeks." Flæd hung her head and did not reply. "Your betrothal to Ethelred displeases you."

"I don't want to go away"—Flæd's face twisted with the sorrow she had fought to hide—"and leave Edward, my books—everything." Her father pinched his brow.

"Flæd," he said at length, "why have you been taught to read?" Sad and bewildered, Flæd looked at him. She tried to answer.

"You decreed it," she said, her lips trembling. "You wrote, 'All the free youth among the English people who have opportunity must be set the task of learning, until they know well how to read English writing.'"

"But why you, Æthelflæd?" the king pressed. She could not think what else to say. "Because you were born into a position of duty," Alfred said so sternly that Flæd shrank down further on her stool. "When you marry Ethelred, Wessex weds Mercia. What I have hoped," he continued, taking her hands with more kindness, "is that my children would help bring back the great English learning lost when the Danes destroyed our libraries." Flæd sat up, trying to follow her father's thoughts.

"I read the Chronicle," she protested, "the lives of the saints, the Rule of Saint Benedict, and the epistles of our English abbots and bishops—everything my tutors bring me."

"And because of this you will help Ethelred govern Mercia with wisdom, I think, and teach your people to love letters." The king stared hard at Flæd to see that she had understood this. "You know that I have given Mercia into Ethelred's charge," he went on, "and that his rule protects not only Mercia but also Wessex from Danish invasion. I do not wish to offend one of Ethelred's most trusted men."

"My warder," Flæd said resentfully, "wears the bands, on his neck and arm, of—"

"He is a person of honor," her father cut her off. The candlelight played over his features as he looked at her critically. "Can you make things right between you?"

Flæd struggled to meet her father's eye. "I want to try," was all she could say.

The bishop and mass priest had returned, stepping softly into the room with the book the king had requested. Alfred surveyed the faces of his advisors before he spoke again.

"I will ask no further questions unless the envoy cannot be persuaded to remain with us. Speak with him tonight, Æthelflæd, and perhaps by morning all will be well."

Father John stepped forward. "Lady, may I accompany you to evening prayer, and see you to your quarters after we have supped? We missed your daughter in the scriptorium today," he explained to the king. "I would like to discuss her lessons."

"Take care, John," Asser remarked acidly. "She has become somewhat slippery." He turned to Alfred. "Can we leave the matter to a girl?"

Alfred considered his advisor's question, and then said to

the bishop, "We will give her this night. Keep a guard with you," he addressed the younger priest, "until she is within her own walls. The two of you may go now. Asser and I will stay a little longer with our Latin."

Father John bowed his assent, and quietly he and Flæd left the king's chambers with one of the royal guards. Strains of the evening psalm came to them as they approached the stone chapel where the service had already begun. John slowed as they neared the entryway. "Lady," he said, holding out his hand to her, "our devotions will wait. Come sit with me before we go in." He led her across the grassy yard and they seated themselves against the chapel's outer wall, which still held some warmth from the afternoon sun. Flæd hugged her knees and laid her cheek against the hem of her tunic, feeling the ache of tears she had been trying not to shed.

"Lady Æthelflæd," said Father John softly beside her, "I have come to think of you as both my student and my friend." Flæd kept her face pressed to her knees. John continued, "I wonder, in your study of the Chronicle, have you discovered the account of Burgred of Mercia?"

Flæd looked up in surprise at the unexpected question. "I do not remember that name," she told him, her throat tight.

"Ah, well, Burgred, as you will someday read, was married to your father's sister. He ruled Mercia as its king," John explained, "for two and twenty winters. In the year 874 the Chronicle records King Burgred's surrender of Mercia to the Danes. He fled to Rome," John said gravely, "where he lived out his years and was buried at Saint Mary's church in the English Schools."

"It is not a happy tale," Flæd said glumly.

"It is not," Father John agreed, "but there is deeper misfortune than what the Chronicle tells. King Burgred was not young. He held his kingdom with the help of his best retainer—a strong thane who led the Mercian army at the borders, where the Danes learned to hate and fear him. When Burgred left his throne, this thane fought on, not knowing his king had gone, not knowing that his own family stood unprotected in the very heart of Mercia." The priest's voice was very quiet now. "Rumors of the king's departure reached the thane's men. They began to desert their commander, who would not believe the reports. The thane still fought, trapped with his dwindling army, refusing to surrender. Until the Danes brought his wife to the battlefield in fetters, and he knew his king had failed him, and he laid down his sword."

"What happened to him?" Flæd asked, appalled.

"He was made a slave," John said, his mellow voice now tight with anger, "and was taken north of the River Humber." John paused a moment, then continued. "When Alfred regained English Mercia, and charged Ethelred with its custody, the chief aldorman and your father sent secret emissaries to the north. They found the thane, bought his freedom, and brought him back to the Mercian court. This man still wears the bands of slavery in memory of his king's betrayal." The priest looked into her face as Flæd drew a startled breath. "Your warder was Burgred's forsaken thane."

Dumbly Flæd stared at her tutor, who nodded to assure her of his story's truth. "Lady," he went on, taking her cold hand in his, "I would say a little more before we enter and pray. When your father bested the Danes one year ago, he called their leaders to feast with him, and with honor offered them a plan for peace." The young priest stood, drawing Æthelflæd up to stand beside him. "I do not ask what has passed between you and the Mercian," he told her. "I have told you something of the man because I think King Alfred's daughter will deal fairly with a person she understands."

Flæd went with John into the softly lit church, where a priest was offering the final prayers of the service. Ælf and Dove came running to her when the liturgy had ended, the smaller girl dancing with impatience at having been still so long. Dove leaned close to her older sister as they made their way toward the kitchens. A bowl of soup cooled, untouched, in front of Flæd as she listened to the little girls tell her how they had hung their new slippers around their necks while they made mud cakes. "She" (Ælf indicated a serving woman who still looked mildly annoyed) had put an end to their game with scrubbing and scolding. "And our shoes were still perfectly clean for prayers," Ælf said with wounded pride, lifting the dirt-caked hem of her gown to display the footwear in question.

"We thought we passed you on the way to the church,"

Dove was saying, "because we saw the Grey Man"—her sisters' name for the Mercian warder.

Ælf looked toward the place where Red usually sat. "Is the Grey Man lost?" she asked with concern.

"He's waiting for us at our chambers," Flæd replied, with a little feeling of dread. "We'll find him there when we go back."

When the sisters had finished eating, Father John and the guard accompanied them through the streets. As their door came into view he stopped. "You may go the rest of the way yourselves," he said to them. "We will watch until you are safely there."

Flæd took her sisters' hands and crossed the street to the entrance, where the Mercian warder sat unmoving in the darkness. Inside she could hear the serving women preparing the room for the night. "Go to bed," she told Ælf and Dove, urging them gently through the doorway. "I'll come in a moment."

Flæd stood in front of her warder, who remained motionless. She looked back at Father John, who raised his hand to her, and then turned to go. Flæd crouched down on the dusty ground facing the Mercian.

"Envoy of Ethelred of Mercia," she said, "I have come to ask your pardon." Flæd swallowed hard and went on. "You are an honored guest of the West Saxon king and his family, and you have broken no trust with Alfred, or with Ethelred." Sitting before her warder with her shoulders bowed, Flæd told him how she had found the hollow atop the mound, and how she had learned to disappear from the grey horses' backs at a gallop. She admitted that she had hidden when he came to find her, just before the three strangers seized her.

Flæd trembled with shame as she said these things. It had been an awful choice to abuse the trust of the man who had dutifully cared for her, who had even tried to soften the burden of his watching with small acts of kindness. But it was worst of all to acknowledge that even after he had saved her, she had continued with her lie.

"Now you know how I wronged you," she said, trying in vain to see his face. "I am even more sorry," she quavered, "because of what you have already suffered." Flæd paused, able to discern no reaction from her warder in the gloom. Then she told him what she had learned that night about his past.

When she had finished, there was a long silence. At last Flæd got to her feet with a deep sense of failure. "The king knows that I am to blame," she said hopelessly. "I will be sorry to see you go." She turned to pass through the doorway.

"Lady." His voice stopped her, rough as broken stone in the blackness. "Before you spoke, I knew I should ask the king's pardon, and offer my poor services again." His voice became a grating whisper. "I couldn't save my wife—she died a slave before they set me free. The Danes killed my son, and no one can tell me what happened to my two daughters.

I don't want," he said with anguish in his hoarse tone, "to lose another person I have promised to protect."

There was a rattle above them as a serving woman unfastened the shutters of a window and pushed them open. Light and children's voices filtered tranquilly into the street. Flæd reached a hand out to the Mercian and braced herself against the doorjamb to help the large man rise.

"How could any enemy harm me," she said, clasping his hand firmly, "as long as I stay with you?"

III
Summer

12

The King's Council

"THE DAGGER IS DANISH."

"The workmanship of the hilt is very like that of the North Welsh craftsmen," Asser announced, turning the knife to look at either side, "but something is not right. . . ."

"Look at the blade," Red said, taking the dagger from him and holding it in a square of light from the council chamber window. He ran his finger carefully along the knife's short edge to the weapon's point. "Its shape is English or Welsh, but look here." He indicated a cloudy mark on the metal just where the blade met the hilt. Asser peered closely at the spot, and then raised his eyes to the king, concern written on his features.

"It is a craftmark," he told Alfred, "nearly scraped away, but there nonetheless. The mark may show the form of some letter, or perhaps another kind of symbol, but this is no English or Welsh character."

"But the men the envoy has described—their faces and their clothes—sound Welsh, perhaps, or even Mercian."

Listening, Flæd sighed. They had been through this conversation again and again with her father's advisors, and it always ended in confusion. No one could say for certain who the attackers had been.

"If you had brought back the body—"

"The girl's safety was more important. We sent a cart. . . ."

"And the body was gone. We have heard."

Suddenly Flæd was impatient. She had sat quietly in her father's chambers, cowed at first by the barrage of questions flung at her warder. But these men were accomplishing nothing. They had never even asked her what she saw when she was alone with her abductors.

"One of them spoke English," she said. The men's faces turned toward her in surprise. "He only spoke it to me. I did not recognize the language they spoke to each other."

"The words I heard were Danish." Red spoke up again. "I learned some of their speech during my time in the Danelaw."

"They threatened me," Flæd went on. "The Mercian envoy may have understood what they said." Her warder pressed his lips together and nodded.

"They planned to . . . to hurt her, then take her away."

"What, then?" a young thane wanted to know. "Why steal the king's daughter? To offend Ethelred? To start another war?"

"We cannot say exactly what these . . . strangers intended," Asser's nasal voice broke in, "but we must seriously consider the possibility of a new threat from the west."

"Perhaps an alliance of Danes and Welshmen," Alfred said thoughtfully, raising an eyebrow at Asser, who was himself Welsh. "I do not think Guthrum"—he named the Danish leader with whom he had drawn up the great treaty one year earlier—"would break his pact with me. But not all his people will be governed by him. Some may have found allies—or at least stolen clothing and equipment, I suppose—across the western border." He addressed the gathering: "We have seen no others after these three?"

"A messenger will bring word of any such sighting," the leader of the royal guard replied.

"What do you make of this, Asser?" Alfred asked, motioning for the bishop to join him at the table. "Are there indeed those among the Welsh who would be Danish allies and bring war to us again?"

Asser folded his hands in front of him. "There are some among the northern Welsh," he replied, "who might wish it so." The bishop looked up sharply from beneath his lowered brows. "Should we not assemble a heavier guard for Lady Æthelflæd? Two to four armed retainers to watch over her until she travels to Mercia?" In her corner Flæd gave a little gasp of dismay.

"King Alfred, a suggestion," said Red. The king waved

her guardian to him, and listened as the envoy spoke quietly into his ear. Moving as close to them as she could, Flæd missed the first words that Red said.

"How long?" she heard her father ask in a low voice.

"Several weeks. I think we have some time before they try again."

"You believe she would be safe?"

"She will not leave me again," Red said with a certainty that made Flæd blush. "I have seen guards corrupted. This way is best."

When Flæd and Red emerged from Alfred's council chambers, the late sunshine of a summer evening filled the street. They walked a little way without speaking.

"What did you say to the king?" Flæd finally asked.

"Wait and see," Red answered.

The next day when Flæd looked up from her Latin translation, she saw with a little shock that her warder had disappeared. In his place sat a young guard she recognized as a sentry from her father's council chambers. But where was Red? Flæd had turned very little of her Latin epistle into English by the time the Mercian envoy reappeared and sent the other guard on his way.

"Lady"—Father John touched her shoulder—"I have been instructed to let you go with the Mercian envoy this afternoon." He looked down at her work. "I see you have your mind on other things today. Well, bring a finished translation in the morning." Gathering up her writing, Flæd began walking toward the door. Edward hissed as she passed him.

"He *left* you today," he said with amazement. "Flæd, where are you going?"

"I don't know," Flæd said with an excited shrug. Edward scowled, and turned back to his tablet.

"Where were you?" Flæd demanded when she reached the scriptorium entrance.

"Went to see the smith," Red replied mysteriously. "Follow me." After a second's pause Flæd hurried after the Mercian envoy, who strode on until they had passed through the gates of the burgh wall. Here he turned and went along the wall until they reached an outcropping at the base of a watch shelter. No guards had been posted here yet, and the place looked deserted to Flæd as she watched her warder poke among the piled stones. He drew out a battered sword of medium length, a leather cap not unlike the one he himself often wore, and a heap of grey metal links which, when held up, proved to be a boy-size shirt of ring mail.

"I told the smith these were for the king's child. He thought I meant Edward," Red told Flæd, "but they will fit you. Let's get started." With a grin Flæd wedged the parchment she had been carrying into a niche of the wall, and began pulling the heavy mail shirt over her tunic.

13

Battle Lessons

In the days that followed, Red would add a dagger and two old shields to the collection of equipment stored in the wall. He brought Flæd to the place every afternoon and, one by one, showed her the use of each weapon. One shield was slightly concave, like a very shallow dish, and Flæd learned that she could use its shape to catch the tip of an opponent's weapon (Red generally used a peeled green staff about the length of a large sword) and push it away from her body, throwing her adversary off balance. The other shield, which had a rounded boss at its center, could turn direct blows into glancing ones—it cast the enemy's weapon away, instead of carrying it. Flæd learned how to position both sorts of shields for various kinds of sword attack, and for the close, vicious assault of a dagger. She learned to keep a shield above her head to protect herself from missiles (usually clods of earth in their practices) while fending off Red's frontal approach with her sword. She learned to move quickly and silently in the surprisingly heavy mail shirt. She learned to shake away the sweat which trickled into her eyes from beneath the leather cap without breaking her concentration from two-handed combat.

Flæd had felt her arms and back growing stronger with each day of practice with the shields. On the day when Red passed the sword into her hand, however, she knew she was still far too weak for true combat. Her boy's weapon was heavy enough to drag her off balance with every stroke, and she could not keep its blunted tip at the level of a man's torso for more than a few seconds. Red brought a post which had been used to brace the unfinished wall and planted it in the middle of their practice ground. He made Flæd hack away at the wood for two full weeks before he ever let her raise her blade against him in practice.

One day Red told Flæd to whistle for the pair of grey horses, which came now whenever she called them even without the bribe of sweet food. He had brought a bridle for each, and he looped the reins of one around Oat's neck as the horse nibbled Flæd's braid.

"See how he feels about a bit in his mouth," Red told her, as he turned to throw the reins of the other bridle across the lowered neck of Apple, who had submitted his forelock for a scratch. Neither of the greys was pleased to feel metal over his tongue after so many months. But after a few head tosses, the bridled horses came with the humans a little way out into the pasture.

"Your friends have grown soft," Red said, running his

hand along Apple's sleek coat. "Strange that no one brought them into the burgh this summer. Well, the two of us will give them some work." Red cupped his hand to support Flæd's knee, and tossed her onto Oat's back. He took Apple's reins and mounted the other horse himself. "Watch carefully," he told her. "Try to do what I do."

Red and Flæd rode side by side. At Red's instruction, they urged their horses into a gallop, and the Mercian leaned to one side and executed a sweeping motion of his sword arm, as if striking at a man on foot with an imaginary blade. Flæd saw him do this, and when he shouted to her, she extended her sword arm and leaned out to mimic Red's motion. Oat veered right, following the pressure of Flæd's near leg and the tug upon his bit as she bent down, and Flæd was nearly thrown. Clutching at Oat's mane and abruptly drawing in his head, she saved herself from a fall, but both she and the horse were breathing hard and rolling their eyes when Red circled back to them.

"Keeping your seat is more important than making your stroke," Red said to her, and before Flæd could tell him that this seemed obvious, he curtly described how she must sit the horse as evenly from the waist down as if she were riding in the usual upright way. Her torso and arm must move separately from the rest of her. When Flæd had listened to this, she urged Oat into a gallop again, and with Red on Apple alongside them shouting corrections, made the leaning stroke without causing a break in her horse's stride. Red had her repeat the exercise twice again, and then asked for the same movement on her opposite side. Flæd did this, more awkwardly, again three times before she and Red returned to the wall.

"Would this not be more easily done from a saddle?" Flæd asked dubiously.

"Yes," Red said briskly, "so you must learn without one."

Red did not bring a saddle to the pasture until more than a week had passed and Flæd could make those two strokes, as well as five others, while holding her practice sword in either hand. From the saddle the exercises were easier at first, until Red began to insist that she reach even further down or out for each imaginary attacker. By the end of three weeks the horses, too, had developed new skills—pivoting and stopping rapidly, ignoring the flash of a blade beside their heads, responding to several new spoken commands.

Red extended their lessons, asking again and again for the maneuvers he had taught her, and watching from horseback as he cantered alongside his laboring student on the long summer afternoons. On fair days the light would stay in the sky well into the evenings, and a few times Red insisted that Flæd continue their drills until long after the day's last prayers and meal had finished. It was almost dark one night when Flæd dismounted after a final galloping pass. Tonight Apple and Oat walked instead of trotting when they were sent off to the herd. Flæd saw Red looking after the two greys with approval, and noted the muscles that had begun to appear beneath their dappled coats. In the dusk she stumbled, catching her foot in a little hole beneath the grass. She suddenly realized how very tired she was. She felt the way the horses had looked, as if she had just enough strength left to make her way home.

"Tomorrow," Red said to her, "I want you to show me your trick of disappearing from a horse's back."

Flæd looked at him in surprise. They had not spoken of Flæd's second escape after that night when Red had agreed to stay, and since they had begun riding the horses again, she had hardly thought of it. Now she did not know what to say. Before they reached the burgh, Red spoke again.

"In battle a horse can be your shield. A riderless horse could even go unnoticed." His voice lowered as they approached the wall. "Danish raiders sit their horses like flies. But I have never seen them vanish like that. If you can fool me," he rumbled, "you'd fool them."

It took Flæd three days to teach Red the skill she had discovered in the pasture that spring. Both of them were thoroughly bruised after the first two afternoons, and Red earned himself nasty scrapes on both elbows when he tried to slip down along Apple's off side with the horse at a run. The horse pulled up, kicking out in complaint against the extra weight yanking on his mane. "Too heavy and too old to hang by my hands and heels from a horse," Red pronounced himself. But the fall did nothing to blunt his sharp comments as he watched her practice.

One morning Flæd woke to the welcome sound of rain on the roof of her quarters. She smiled with relief. No tumbles in the grass today, she thought happily. Maybe my sore shoulder will finally begin to heal. But Red met her at the scriptorium entrance with the mail shirt in his hand.

"The king has excused you from the classroom," Red told her, handing her the ring mail and producing a small pouch of hard bread and dry cheese, which he divided between them. "Eat this. We have a long walk ahead."

Wearing the mail shirt and carrying a leather satchel which Red had slung over her shoulders (and which felt as if it were filled with lead), Flæd slogged off into the rain behind the Mercian. At first Flæd shivered, but her sodden clothes were hot and sticking to her skin beneath the mail shirt as she labored to keep up with her warder. Following Red, she left the burgh and crossed the pasture to the little wood and the forked ford in the river. The water was only thigh-deep this late in summer, and Flæd did not bother to remove her sopping shoes or kilt up her already dripping skirt before they crossed.

Instead of turning toward the marsh when they reached the other side, Red headed deeper into the wood, following a path which, Flæd thought impatiently, looked as if it had no nearer destination than the western hills where the sun set each night. Four hours later she found herself slipping exhaustedly in the hillside mud of the same path, which had indeed taken them to the western hills. The leather strap of the bag she carried had pressed her mail shirt hard against her body until welts had risen on her shoulder and hip beneath her wet clothes. Her hands were swollen from the long walk, and wrinkled with rain. Mud had seeped into her shoes, and the grit had rubbed her toes and heels until even the soft leather felt painful on her feet.

Flæd had asked Red no questions—it took all the breath she had to keep pace with him. Red in turn had exchanged no words with her, except to call out a direction when their path met another. They had travelled through woodland and across open areas of scrub, skirting marshes and crossing three small streams. As they began to climb the hill, trees closed around them again. The thick trunks of oaks and horse chestnuts crowded close to the winding path, and rain dripped through the thick leaves.

Flæd slipped again, falling to her knees. She panted on all fours, and willed herself to rock back onto her feet. Then she felt a large hand lifting her under one arm.

"This way," said Red, leading her off the path into the bracken. "We'll make camp." In a dense ring of trees they found a bit of ground that was almost dry, and Red lit a tiny, smoking fire from the least damp of the twigs and leaves Flæd brought to him. From his pack Red drew two tight rolls of oiled cloth, one of which he spread on the slope at the foot of two trees. The other he secured between two branches a little way above them, blocking the drizzle which made its way through the leaves. A tiny clay cooking pot came next from his satchel, and Red filled this from his waterskin and set it in the sparse coals on one side of the fire. Into the pot he put three small pieces of dried meat, and a handful of hairy leaves he had gathered at the last stream they had crossed. "Comfrey," he told Flæd, "to keep away the chill."

Sitting beneath the sheltering cloth, they took turns sipping the hot brew from the single cup Red passed between them. Flæd's skin felt numb with tiredness. Her legs ached to the bone, and in the morning she knew she would find them stiff and much more painful.

"There's a blanket in your satchel," Red told her, and she opened her pack and found a dark woolen cover to spread over herself. Beneath it she found five large river stones.

"Why?" she demanded, showing Red the inside of her bag.

"You carried no weapons, no shield, and no rations," Red responded. "The stones gave you some of that weight." Flæd thought about this for a moment. She pulled the blanket around her shoulders and felt the steam of her drying clothes rising through the mail shirt she still wore.

"Today you have tried to show me how a soldier travels on foot," Flæd ventured, voicing an idea which had been growing in her mind throughout the day. She was rewarded with a nod from her warder. Flæd thought back to her questions on the last night of the king's council. What had her guardian said to the king? She believed she could guess now—Red had told her father he would teach her to defend herself.

"We will go back tomorrow?" she asked the Mercian at last.

"They expect us by midday," Red assented. Shyly, Flæd hesitated again before saying more to her warder. She wanted to tell him that she understood these lessons after so many weeks, and to ask him another question—one she had wondered about from the day they had met.

"I . . . I could fight those attackers along with you now," she said to him at last.

"Maybe you could," he answered. Flæd chewed her lip, then went on.

"Your name, Red—is that the name your parents gave you?"

"No," Red answered, a wariness creeping into his voice. "People called me Red when I fought—before I lost my family." Firelight glinted on the drops that hung from the edge of the cloth above them, and flickered in changing shadows across the Mercian's face. Flæd clenched her hands together beneath the blanket.

"They called you Red for the color of your sword in battle," she said with terrible certainty, "for the blood of enemies you spilt on the battlefield, where wolves and carrion birds came to feed upon the dead." She shot a solemn look at her warder, and saw that Red was smiling.

"The name was for my head, that's all." He removed the close-fitting leather cap he wore and bent down so that the flames shone on his short hair. In the firelight, as near to her warder as she had ever been, Flæd peered at the familiar grey and white bristles of her warder's cropped head. "Look hard," Red instructed, "I'm like an old strawberry roan horse." And then she saw them: Among the peppering of grey and white, a few rust-colored hairs. Flæd felt her face grow hot, but then before she could stop herself, she began to laugh. From beside her came a low chuckle—Red was laughing, too.

Message to Mercia

"Who is that?"

Flæd, Edward, and Red stood atop the newly finished rampart encircling the burgh, looking out over the great pasture toward the river. At the edge of the marsh, clusters of cotton sedges raised white tufts like hares' tails to the sky, and among these tussocks a man and a horse were picking their way toward the river.

"It's Edric," Edward said, naming one of Alfred's young retainers. "He has just such a dark bay horse."

"No, Grimbald, I think," Flæd replied, squinting into the distance. Bishop Asser had lately sent the young Frankish monk on an errand to a neighboring abbey, and Grimbald would have followed the river's course to this ford on his return journey.

"It's a Mercian," grunted Red. Flæd looked over at him, a question showing in her face. "The crest of his helmet," Red told her, "and the decoration of his horse's bridle." Flæd looked back at the approaching man and horse, who had

reached the river and were splashing onto the near bank
after their ford. Faintly she could make out a glint of interlacing metalwork on the horse's cheekstrap when the bay
tossed its head. The central ridge of the rider's helmet reared
up above his forehead into the shape of an animal. Red, Flæd
realized, must have recognized the workmanship of his
homeland.

"Why would another Mercian come to our burgh?" Edward wondered.

"He has ridden hard," Red replied, still peering out over
the pasture. "He may be a messenger." The three of them
continued to watch as the rider reached the entryway of the
burgh wall, and hailed the watchmen posted there. The men
spoke together for a moment, and then the visitor was let
through and pointed in the direction of the royal council
chambers.

"Let's follow!" Edward said excitedly, scrambling past Red
on his way to the stairs. At the foot of the wall Wulf uncurled
himself and yawned, wagging his tail in greeting as Edward
descended. Flæd looked at her guardian.

"You are Ethelred's envoy," she said. "Shouldn't you
greet this Mercian?" When Red nodded his assent, she hurried down the steps after her brother.

Outside the king's council room they found the bay
horse, reins thrown over onto the ground, neck drooping.
Edward stroked the animal's sweat-crusted side while saying
a few low words, at which the horse swiveled back one tired

ear. "I will ask if I can take him to the stables," Edward told them, and quickly disappeared into the room. A moment later he was back, happily gathering up the reins. "They want you inside," he said as he turned to go with the horse, Wulf pacing along dutifully at heel. They want Red, not me, Flæd thought. But Red motioned for her to lead the way into the king's council chambers, and so she and her warder both entered.

A chair had been brought for the Mercian visitor, and placed before the king's table, where the man had already been served food and drink. The man sat uneasily in front of the king and Bishop Asser, and when he saw Red come into the room, his agitation increased. He stood abruptly, bowing his head to the Mercian envoy.

"Greetings, Cenwulf," Red said. "You had a hard ride."

"I did, my lord," Cenwulf replied, "and nothing must delay my message." He turned back to Alfred. "Two dawns ago, at the western border near Wiogoraceaster, our riders encountered two horsemen in Welsh dress. From a distance these men returned our greeting. Then when we approached, they rode away. We did not see their faces, but"—here the man paused, meeting Alfred's attentive gaze with his own level stare—"those of us who have met the Danes often in battle think these riders bore themselves not like our Welsh neighbors to the west, who are often small men, but like the taller heathen settlers of the Danelaw." The man's face had flushed, and at his belt his fingers played upon the short dagger he had worn into the council room. "The next night two Mercian border watchmen were found dead, one strangled, one with a knife between his ribs. I know we have not met before, King Alfred, but when your aldorman Ethelred posted me at Wiogoraceaster, he commanded me to ride first to your court with news of trouble, and then to go on with haste to Lunden. I hope you will trust me with some message for Ethelred. He will want to know your wishes."

"I can vouch for this man's judgment," came Red's gruff voice. He stepped forward and laid his hand on Cenwulf's shoulder. "He was with me when we fought the Danes in Burgred's Mercia. All of us learned the look of our enemy well."

"He should rest now," Alfred replied. "Your horse is in our stables," he said to the weary rider, "fed and cared for. My people will show you a bed and fresh clothes." The king stood. "Cenwulf of Mercia, I thank you for your message." With another bow Cenwulf stiffly left the room.

"More evil signs! Will you not agree that your daughter should stay well inside the burgh, where all your men can protect her?" Asser pounded a fist on the table. "I do not understand this arrangement of yours." He glared from the king to Red. Alfred turned to the Mercian envoy.

"Is she ready?" the king asked.

"Almost," Red answered him. "Another week of work." Alfred sat thinking for a moment, his face half covered with one of his hands. When he looked up, it was Flæd's eye he sought.

"Cenwulf is right: Ethelred needs to know what we have learned," he said. Flæd tensed—she and her father had not spoken of the Mercian aldorman since the night of her rescue.

"We have learned very little," Asser put in dryly. "We have seen tall Welshmen who speak like Danes, and have perhaps found a Danish blade disguised as Welsh."

"I would rather meet with Ethelred here than send messages asking for his advice," Alfred went on, still speaking to Flæd. "However, I do not think that he should come here openly for parley."

"But surely," the bishop interrupted again, his eyes lighting with possibility as he suddenly understood the king's idea, "he may come to this burgh to greet his future bride, and to feast with her royal family! His absence at the announcement of Lady Æthelflæd's betrothal might be seen as an insult to your daughter," Asser continued with mock seriousness, "did he not honor the lady with at least one visit before she comes to him in Mercia." Alfred tapped his lips with a long finger.

"Cenwulf will continue on to Lunden," he declared at last, "and privately inform Ethelred of our desire to meet with him. But the people of Lunden will learn only that he bears a message, written by the hand of Lady Æthelflæd, asking her betrothed to visit her. Flæd, you would like to meet the chief aldorman of Mercia?" His tone made the words a question, and Flæd groped awkwardly for an answer.

"I would like to meet him," she replied slowly, "and—and hear his advice in the council chamber." Her response brought a smile from her father.

"You ask very little of this man who would be your husband," the king pointed out. "Many brides would crave sweeter words than the advice of an alderman to his king." Flæd felt a flush of embarrassment and confusion. Scowling, she tried to stand straighter beside Red.

"I will write the letter," she said.

Late that night Flæd sat in the scriptorium, alone except for Red, laboring over the last words of her brief message to Ethelred. Painstakingly, she had chosen each phrase of the request, writing them out on her wax tablet before she inked her quill and began to shape the letters on a sheet of parchment.

Now she made the final descending stroke of her last word, and centered a dot between the rulings above and below her last line of letters to show that the writing was complete. She needed only to put her name upon the document, but somehow this was the most difficult moment in her odd assignment. The task her father had given her had made her feel, for just an hour or so, as if she were a part of his own trusted circle of advisors. Now as she looked at what she had written, that feeling faded.

I wasn't in their circle when they decided upon my betrothal, Flæd bridled, and when I go to Mercia, I will go alone, without Father, without John or Bishop Asser, without any of them. Asking me to write one letter doesn't change that. The resentment she had felt from the moment her father had told her of Ethelred's proposal filled her again, stiffening her hand above the fresh ink of her message. Just write your name, she told herself grimly, and it will be finished. Flæd took a breath. She tried to imagine who she was to Ethelred, and to the people of Mercia. At last she drew the straight lines of her name's initial capital letter, and signed the message "Æthelflæd, daughter of Alfred, King."

"That is well written," said a voice at her shoulder, making Flæd jump. Father John stood beside her table looking at the parchment in the yellow light of the two candles she had brought from her father's council room. "Perhaps I will make a name for myself in Mercia as the teacher of their lord's scholar bride. Your father," he continued, ignoring Flæd's black look, "told me of his plan, and asked if I would come to help you. But you have done well without me. This will be a fine introduction for the Mercian people to their new West Saxon lady."

"Her mother is Mercian," Red's voice grated from the shadows at the end of the bench. He stood and came into the candlelight. "The people of Lunden remember Ealhswith."

"True enough," said Father John, with a nod to the large man. Thoughtfully, he turned back to Flæd. "Some people of Mercia will see your marriage as a homecoming, Lady. That is strange, is it not? To come home to a place you have never seen?"

It is not more strange than betrothal to a man I have never seen, Flæd fretted as she and Red walked together through the streets, carrying the letter to the king. Ethelred, her future husband. For the last several weeks Flæd had tried to think of the marriage as her father had explained it: Mercia uniting with Wessex. Learning restored to the English people. But more and more she was reminded that she was promised in marriage to a *person*. She knew little enough of him, and what would he think of a girl who read about battles in books and was learning to cut down an enemy from horseback? A gawky girl with ink-stained hands and dust in her hair? Trudging beside Red, she breathed in the calming tang of summer hay. At least I did not blot, she comforted herself.

Cenwulf would not wait for morning to begin his ride to Lunden. Ethelred must have the news from the border along with the lady's letter as soon as possible, he told the king, who tried to convince him to rest a little longer. With a fresh mount and fair weather, he should reach the Mercian seat in a day.

Before the first sign of dawn, however, Cenwulf knew he had made a mistake—he could barely stay upright on the vigorous horse they had lent him. An hour of sleep, he told himself as he tied the horse and made a bed of dry leaves, then a hard ride the rest of the way.

He did not stir when a hand brushed past his neck and

drew the letter from between his sleeping fingers. He never heard the knife slip under the royal seal.

The eyes that read the girl's writing narrowed. Watching this road for travellers from the West Saxon court had proved worthwhile, just as expected. Here was another opportunity to toy with Alfred, more promising than their attempt to take the girl in the spring. It was always helpful, the reader reflected, when victims left the safety of their homes, carrying money and riding fine horses. Plunder tended to encourage even a cowardly force of men.

With great delicacy the letter was returned—the Mercians would simply think the journey had loosened the seal. Ethelred would come as requested. For now, thought the figure, fingering the knife with regret, this messenger must be allowed to live.

15

Waiting

"DEFEND YOUR OPEN SIDE," RED BARKED. HE REWARDED Flæd's distraction with a slap from the flat of the dull practice blade. Flæd set her jaw and came at her warder again. With surprise, she felt him return her attack with a vicious sweep which knocked her off her feet. She grasped the hand he offered and hauled herself up, breathing hard.

"You will never be as strong as a larger man you meet in battle," Red said to her as she rubbed the stinging fingers which had held her sword. "That poem you read in the marsh, what does it say about the woman-monster?"

Flæd tried to recall the lines. "The poem says, 'Her strength—the battle-strength of a woman—was less than a male, whose sword can shear through a helmet.' "

"But she was still terrible," Red said.

Flæd nodded. "She was cunning. She attacked when they did not expect her, and later she fought in her own lair, a place she knew well."

Red leaned on his sword. "I'm stronger. You're smaller,

quicker, and lighter. Now, find a way to beat me with a sword."

They readied their weapons. Three times more Flæd found herself thrown on her back by Red's hard, direct strokes. The fourth time, Flæd dropped to the ground just before their blades met, rolling under Red's slash and scrambling to her feet behind him as he stumbled to find his balance. Before he could turn she had touched the blunted edge of her blade against his neck. "Good," was all her warder said. And then, "Again."

Flæd's bones still ached from the lesson when she was prodded awake by a serving woman the next morning. She listened groggily to the instructions her mother had sent. She was not expected at the scriptorium today, or in the practice field. It was time to choose the gifts she would take to Ethelred. More preparations for going away, Flæd thought, burying her face in her pillow. But after breakfast she dutifully found her mother in the buildings where the burgh's dry stores were kept.

Ealhswith had come before her, and was kneeling in the center of a room filled with draped and folded cloth. Before her stood little Ælf, her hair a bright tangle around her shoulders, wearing a nearly finished gown of dark blue.

"Flæd!" her little sister cried, and started to come toward her.

"No, no, stay here, little one." Her mother stopped the girl with a hand on her wrist. "We must shorten this, or you will catch your new shoe on the hem and fall." Ealhswith bent to her measurements again, but Ælf twisted her head around to speak to Flæd over her shoulder.

"I do have new shoes, Flæd." She thrust one out from under the skirt and held her foot out for her older sister to admire its oiled leather slipper.

"Ælf," the queen chastened, "two feet on the ground. We're almost finished."

Flæd knelt down in front of her youngest sister and listened to a flurry of excited words as the little girl told her about the new clothing they had chosen that morning. A fresh shift and tunic for play, this blue dress for feasting days, stiff new shoes which did not crimp the toes like the old ones. . . . Flæd let Ælf's high, quick voice patter on, realizing how little time she had spent with her sisters since the spring. At meals she was always in a hurry, rushing to her lessons, or to practice with Red. When she returned to their quarters her sisters were often already sleeping. Even if Dove and Ælf were awake, Flæd usually fell into her own bed too tired for anything more than cuddling the little ones beside her until the serving women took them back to their pallets. She had begun to lose her sisters even before she left the burgh, Flæd thought mournfully.

"Flæd!" Dove came running from behind a stack of cloth. "Look at *my* new gown." Flæd inspected the thin figure, who plucked up the sides of her dress and held them out for her older sister's admiration. The rich cloth of the gown was dark brown, trimmed at the neck and sleeves with a braided cord of even darker wool. It was very much like the clothing of the nuns Dove admired, Flæd could not help noticing.

"This new gown covers those tiny bird ankles of yours at last," Flæd said, tweaking Dove's braid before her sister disappeared again among the stacks of cloth. Ealhswith shook her head.

"You'd think her a novice in training among the abbey's sisters already," the queen said, "were she a few winters older." Ealhswith bent to the hem of the blue gown one last time, and then quickly stripped the dress over the head of her smaller daughter, who squeaked with surprise and then giggled to find herself standing clad only in new shoes and a white shift. "Put on your other tunic and go play with Dove," her mother told her. "Flæd and I must look at some cloth."

The queen turned to Flæd. "Come see what has just arrived." She led Flæd to a place near the door of the room, where morning sunlight streamed in under the lintel. The light formed a patch of glowing red on the table where a fine cloth had been unfolded for inspection. "This is wool spun, dyed, and woven by a woman I knew in Wintanceaster," Ealhswith told her, "when we lived there just after your birth. See, it is very fine. And what color!"

"A royal color," Flæd agreed, fingering the dense, even threads. "It will make fine robes for the king."

"She sent this to us," Ealhswith replied, "after the announcement of your betrothal. It is a royal gift, but not for Alfred."

Flæd withdrew her hand from the beautiful stuff. "It would look as wrong on me as—as scarlet feathers on a sparrow," she said darkly.

"Perhaps you could wear it," Ealhswith said, drawing her daughter close, "for the woman who made the cloth. She held you when you were born, and sends this in tribute to the babe who has grown up worthy of such a gift." Ealhswith turned to face Flæd. "You might wear this red in Mercia," she said, "for the sake of a good West Saxon weaver, and in memory of the royal West Saxon family she seeks to honor."

Flæd looked at the bright cloth a moment longer, then nodded. With her mother she also chose a dark green wool, and added a cloth the color of ripe wheat for other gowns. These they gave to the woman who would make the garments in the coming weeks. Ælf and Dove had spread a length of coarse linen between the tables, and Ealhswith and Flæd left them whispering in their tent, attended by a servant who began measuring out Flæd's new cloth nearby.

From the royal family's stores Flæd and her mother picked out carved wooden bowls, leather bottles of wine, a polished horn for drinking, and a bright golden cup not as large as the silver one Alfred passed to his guests, but intricately decorated with interlacing branches which seemed to grow from the vessel's slender stem. They chose a heavy ring with a smoothly polished green gem for the hand of

Ethelred of Mercia. Three chests filled with silver coins bearing Alfred's image would come from the treasury, as well. Last of all, they stood in the blacksmith's rooms and examined the linked rings of the armor that hung there, the clean blades of the swords the craftsman had forged. "How tall is the Mercian aldorman?" the smith asked, but they didn't know. They would have to come back another time, the queen said.

It was late in the day when they had finished, and Flæd walked with her mother to the door of the queen's quarters. Ealhswith stopped outside and looked at Flæd, smoothing the hair back from her daughter's face.

"Still sad, little bird?" she asked. A lump rose in Flæd's throat as her mother used the name she had called her when she was a very small girl.

"Ethelred . . . I don't even know—" She could not finish, but the queen seemed to understand.

"It is hard, the waiting," her mother said.

"Did you want to come here, to be a queen?" Flæd asked her mother in a rush.

"I hoped that I would find a peaceful place, a quiet life in Wessex," Ealhswith replied evenly. "I hoped that Alfred would help bring peace to Mercia through our marriage. The Danes had made my home dangerous."

"Then you were not like me," Flæd choked. "I already had a quiet life, with my books, our weaving, before the betrothal—before those men tried to take me."

"Your father has worked to keep your home peaceful, but he has been at war every year of his kingship until this last one." Her mother shook her head. "Alfred loves contemplation and the solace of his books, just as you do. Do you remember what I told you at the end of the winter, just before your betrothal was announced?"

" 'We do not know what we may become,' " Flæd murmured.

"Your father, who would rather have been a scholar, became a warrior, and a good king." The queen took Flæd's face between her hands. "What will you become, I wonder, now that you must give up your quiet life?" For a long moment Ealhswith stood gazing into her daughter's troubled eyes. "You chose well today, Æthelflæd," she said at last. "If I must part with my eldest daughter, it makes me glad to send her back to the place of my own birth with treasure. May you find happiness there," the queen finished, kissing Flæd on the cheek and withdrawing into her rooms.

Happiness, thought Flæd, wanting to take comfort in her mother's words. A man who is a stranger, and a place I have never seen—if I can't imagine these, how can I imagine happiness?

But still she tried. He could even come today, she brooded the next morning. A wagon trip to Lunden might take two or three days, but for a rider on horseback, the journey might be as short as one. Knowing this, Flæd found herself peering out toward the river, looking out over the buttercups scattered amid the long grass like golden coins. A messenger will arrive to tell us Ethelred of Mercia is coming. What will Ethelred look like? What will he say? How will he look at me?

When the messenger comes, she decided, I will wash the dust out of my hair, and put on a new gown so that I am ready to greet Ethelred when he follows. I will try to remember what Father John has told me about Mercia.

We gave Cenwulf a good horse. A messenger will soon be on his way. . . .

Then Ethelred will come.

16

Ethelred

AT TWILIGHT THE MERCIAN MESSENGER ARRIVED. SITTING ON her bed Flæd heard the far-off sentries loudly hail a rider, and with a hammering in her chest she listened until the sound of tired hoofbeats passed not far from her door. A day and a half for the messenger to ride to Lunden—Flæd quickly tallied the time—a day of discussion between Ethelred and his thanes, and then the messenger's swift journey back to say that Ethelred is coming. Her heart was still racing when Red spoke softly into the room.

"Lady, we should cross to your father's council chamber." Flæd glanced at her sleeping sisters, and then inspected her own plain clothing. She had been patching a hole in her leather shoe by rushlight, at a place where her toe had worn through the slipper in the rough footing of the meadow. Her shabbiness wouldn't matter for this meeting with the rider from Mercia—she and Red would stand off in a corner to hear what news the man had brought of Ethelred's plans. Then they would come back here for sleep, that was all. Quietly she pulled on the half-mended shoe and its mate, and put out her lamp.

Light spilled out onto the street from the entryway to Alfred's council chamber, and the sentry by the door motioned Flæd and her warder inside. The king was speaking with the messenger, and he broke off to greet Flæd as she and Red came in.

"Æthelflæd, this rider brings word that your letter was welcome to the people of Lunden. It seems that Ethelred began his journey almost as soon as our message reached him. The chief aldorman of Mercia is at our gates."

Flæd felt her stomach knotting. She looked quickly at Red, who had already inclined his ear to the doorway. Sounds of a large party approaching had begun to echo in from the street. Bishop Asser and Father John, speaking quietly to each other, entered the council chamber and came to stand beside the king. The noise of hooves and jingling gear of many horses came closer, until Flæd could see movement just beyond the light of the entryway. One man's voice called out a command to halt, and the noise changed, as horses snorted and booted feet dropped to the ground.

Swiftly Flæd stepped back beside her warder into the shadowy corner by the door just as the sentry spoke his first words to the party of newcomers. She could not quite make out the sentences they exchanged, but a moment later the sentry's mailed shoulders filled the doorway.

"Ethelred, Chief Aldorman of Mercia, greets King Alfred," the guard announced. He stepped back, and the Mercian aldorman strode into the room, accompanied by four other men who arranged themselves behind him when he stopped in front of Alfred.

"Ethelred," Alfred said with a smile, coming forward to clasp the aldorman's forearm in greeting, "we bid you welcome to our burgh."

"Burgh!" Ethelred exclaimed, opening his mouth in a laugh. "From the look of the wall we passed, I'd call this a king's *tun*." Ethelred used the word for heavily fortified settlements which defended whole communities when enemies threatened.

"Nonsense, my friend," Alfred responded with a laugh of his own. "This is only a humble burgh, where my family enjoys peace and simple living." Flæd could see Ethelred's profile as he drew breath for another retort. The Mercian aldorman looked a few years younger than her father, but was less finely drawn than the king. He had removed his helmet before he entered Alfred's rooms, and Flæd could see that his hair was light brown, almost a bronze color in the candlelight of Alfred's council chamber. His face looked broad and square from Flæd's vantage, and the wrinkles of a smile appeared at the corner of his eye as he spoke again.

"You may call this king's *tun* a burgh if you wish. Certainly we have come here from Mercia with no other thought than to greet your royal daughter in the beautiful West Saxon countryside."

"Greet her, then," said Alfred, with a sly look on his mobile face. "Chief Aldorman of Mercia," he pronounced, stepping around Ethelred and his men, and taking the startled Flæd by the hand, "here is Lady Æthelflæd of Wessex." In spite of her own dismay, Flæd could not help noticing that surprise had frozen Ethelred's features at the moment she stood before him. She was keenly aware of her rumpled gown, of the fuzzy hairs that had escaped her braid and trailed into her face, of the half-mended shoe which showed a pink flash of her toe through the remaining hole. She hid this foot behind the other.

"Lady Æthelflæd," the Mercian aldorman spoke, regaining his composure, "your message was most gladly received in Lunden. I am honored to greet you in your father's burgh." Ethelred placed special emphasis on this last word, showing a trace of his former smile, and dropped to one knee.

"You are welcome here," Flæd said softly, finding her own voice. She bowed her head to the aldorman, and then stepped back beside her warder. Ethelred broke into a grin when he saw Red standing there. He strode forward and laid his hand on Red's shoulder.

"It is very good to see you again," he said warmly. Ethelred looked over at Alfred. "My retainer has insured the safety of Lady Æthelflæd?" he asked.

"He has indeed met the challenge of that task," Alfred replied, eyeing Red and Flæd with a half-smile. "Ethelred," he continued, "you and your men have had a long and weary ride. Take your horses to our stables. We will send food to your quarters, where you may rest yourselves until morning when we will meet here to talk again."

"I trust we will also find time to celebrate this happy visit?" Ethelred asked with a quirk to his mouth.

"Tomorrow we shall feast," Alfred agreed.

"In a day or two my horses will be rested," Ethelred mused innocently. "I had thought, perhaps, a race?"

"I have not forgotten your boasts," the king told him. "I would like to see if these Mercian horses are as fast as you claim. Yes, we will announce it. The next day, a race between West Saxon and Mercian riders."

When Ethelred and his men had gone, Red and Flæd were sent to their rest. Flæd was still reeling with the evening's surprises, and was glad to walk through the cool night air with only the familiar company of Red and the masspriest John, who went with them.

"I believe Ethelred has raced here before," Father John said as they walked.

"Ethelred has raced *here*?" she asked in surprise. John nodded, and Flæd thought she could detect amusement upon his face in the starlight.

"If your father has kept this story from you, it is not because of modesty," her tutor told her. "Ethelred bested fine riders who had the swiftest mounts of the West Saxon stables."

"Here?" Flæd asked again.

"You have never noticed it, then?" John said with curiosity. "It has not been used since just before your father brought his family to this burgh." Flæd shook her head, still not understanding. "The raised ground around the edge of the meadow?" John asked. "Edward tells me you walk there to avoid the winter floods." Suddenly Flæd could picture it— the vast oval of worn, elevated earth ringing the pasture. A racecourse. "Your father passed through this settlement with a group of West Saxon and Mercian retainers, Ethelred among them," Father John was saying. "The races they ran against each other here gave them a little respite from the wars. Perhaps that happy time encouraged your father to come back here with his wife and children."

Ethelred had raced horses in their own pasture against Flæd's father. This did not surprise her after what she had just seen in Alfred's chambers. The aldorman had laughed and blustered. He and the king had warmed each other with their banter. He was her father's true friend, she felt more certain after tonight. But he cooled when he saw me, she remembered. We are still strangers to each other. And perhaps, a little voice nagged, he did not like what he saw.

Well, Flæd thought with a toss of her head, perhaps I am not sure I liked what I saw. In the morning, wearing her good clothes and her full dignity, she intended to have a second look at Ethelred of Mercia.

17

The Race

"WE WILL NOT STAND BY WHILE DANES CROSS OUR BORDER!" Ethelred insisted.

"Chief Aldorman," Asser said patiently, "we do not suggest leaving Mercia defenseless. But we must choose the proper time and place to move against the enemy."

Flæd rubbed her eyes wearily. She and Red had listened all morning while Ethelred and his advisors deliberated with Alfred and Asser. The men reviewed all they had learned from the border guards. They questioned Red closely again, probing his memory of Danish battle tactics. Now they had settled in to argue over what to do next.

Ethelred had seemed surprised to see Flæd waiting in the council room when he arrived that morning. After a moment's hesitation the large man had smiled politely to her and bowed. Then he seemed to forget about her, turning instead to her warder and questioning him about his stay in Wessex. In fact there had been very little for Flæd to do at the council table that morning, and she had settled back further on her bench as the voices of the men rose in debate. Beside her Red was nearly as silent, speaking out only when he was addressed. Flæd tugged at a thread which dangled from her sleeve.

"And would you have us risk the lives of innocents, who understand nothing of this threat? Risk the lives of our children? The life of one so delicate as Lady Æthelflæd here, who will travel to Mercia only a week or so behind my own party if you send me back now?" Ethelred said heatedly. There was a small silence while he glared around the room. Ethelred's frown deepened when he saw Alfred smiling, and noticed that even Red's expression had lightened.

"Forgive us, Ethelred," Alfred said to him, "for your argument is serious. Like you, we have thought my daughter delicate. She has begun to convince us otherwise." Alfred paused, considering his next words carefully. "Ethelred, I need your presence in Lunden again as quickly as possible— our talks have convinced me that our Mercian holdings must not be left vulnerable in any way. I could send my daughter with you now, it is true"—(Flæd caught her breath in alarm)—"but I have promised her these last few days with her family. Of course we will send her with a suitable company of armed retainers. I have confidence that Æthelflæd's own hardheadedness will bring her safely to Lunden, in the watchful company of my men, and of your own valued thane"—the king nodded at Red—"just as we had planned before I called you here." Flæd looked away from the table, abashed, but not before she had seen Ethelred color with embarrassment. Then Father John's gentle voice sounded across the room.

"We should not wonder at Lady Æthelflæd's boldness," her tutor said. "Her mother, after all, is Mercian." Flæd could feel some of the tension ease in the room as Ethelred and his retainers acknowledged the compliment. She wished herself ten days' march away as Ethelred cautiously began speaking again.

When they left the council room, Flæd slipped ahead quickly to walk with Father John, avoiding Ethelred, who had stayed to exchange a few more words with the king.

"Thank you for speaking," she said to her tutor. "The aldorman seems—he was close to anger today."

"He is passionate about the land he governs, I would say," John replied mildly, "and he has not judged you properly, but that would be a poor reason to spoil these talks. I only reminded the Mercians of a fact they already knew." He looked at Flæd curiously. "You find the aldorman . . . unpleasant?" Flæd looked down.

"I don't know what to think of him," she muttered. "He doesn't seem to care much about me."

"Why is it," Father John mused, catching the eye of Red, who strode along with them, "that people often fail to see what a woman can do? It is always true of the holy women whose lives are written in our books." He threw up his hands in mock pleading. "To everyone's surprise Saint Helen, mother of Constantine, discovered the true cross." Flæd felt the shadow of a smile cross her lips.

"Who knew that Saint Juliana could wrestle a devil to the ground?" she joined in, feeling a little better.

"There is a poem which I haven't shown you yet," the priest went on, "in which a single Hebrew woman defeats the entire Assyrian army. While no one is looking"—he arched an eyebrow at Flæd—"she cuts off the general's head. Please, Lady, spare the aldorman if he makes himself difficult again." Flæd had to laugh.

That night Flæd sat beside Ethelred in the great hall. She wore the new straw-colored gown she would take with her to Mercia, and around her throat lay the necklace of twisted gold which Ethelred had sent to mark their betrothal.

"The necklace looks well upon you, Lady," Ethelred told her, a bit stiffly. "Did my other gifts please you?"

"They are all very fine," Flæd said shyly. "I . . . my mother is keeping them for me until I bring them to Lunden."

"Lunden is not so far from here," Ethelred said. (Yes, I know, Flæd thought to herself, a little offended—I have seen it on the map.) "But a wagon is never comfortable," the aldorman continued. "I fear you will find it a longer and less agreeable journey than my hasty ride to your father's burgh—from sunrise to just after sunset, we rode."

"I can ride, my lord aldorman," Flæd said slowly, trying to understand what Ethelred meant, "even if my party must come to Mercia more slowly than you and your men came here, I can sit a horse for several days."

"I wouldn't think it wise for you to come mounted into Mercia," Ethelred replied. "Danish raiders ride like demons. Surely you would be safest with the guarded wagons bringing your goods. You have not understood the dangers we spoke of in the council room. . . ."

Flæd felt a hot stab of anger. A small part of her realized that Ethelred was trying to be kind. A much less pleasant part of her wanted to recite all the Danish military history she had learned from the Chronicle. Instead, she shut her lips tightly and stared hard at her food. Ethelred seemed not to notice that their conversation had ended badly. He turned to Alfred on his other side and began a bantering speech which soon had the king laughing. Alfred stood to address the gathering.

"We welcome you, West Saxons and Mercians, to our hall tonight. Our guest, Ethelred, chief aldorman of Mercia, has just renewed his old boast, saying that Mercia breeds swifter horses and bolder riders than does Wessex." The king raised his hand for silence as the noise rose in the hall again. "We must treat our Mercian guests with nothing less than respect," he continued, "but it would be unkind to let them leave our burgh believing a falsehood. We must show them that they are wrong in this opinion." There was laughter in the crowd now, and Flæd heard several good-natured jabs directed at the Mercian retainers scattered around the hall.

Alfred raised his voice to be heard above the gathered people. "I propose a race in the great pasture tomorrow. All West
Saxon riders who wish to meet the Mercian challenge may
come, and Ethelred has promised that he and his men will be
waiting there for us."

There was talk of the race all around as the king and his
guests at the high table stood to go. As Flæd filed past the
bench where her brothers and sisters sat, she leaned over to
hiss in Edward's ear, "Meet me at my chamber tonight."

He came much later that evening, and found Flæd sitting
on her bed plaiting her hair and thinking hard. "Flæd," he
whispered, slipping beneath the door hanging and coming to
sit beside her, "have you looked at the Mercian horses?" She
shook her head. "They're the best I've seen," he told her
worriedly. "Father John told me Ethelred won the last time
he and father raced."

"He said the same thing to me," Flæd responded, "but I
don't think Father plans to ride tomorrow. Anyhow, this race
will be different." Speaking very softly to keep from waking
her sisters, Flæd told Edward what she had in mind. When
she had finished, her brother could scarcely sit still.

"But will it really work?" he wanted to know.

"A fresh horse, a light rider—it will work." She put her
hand on Edward's shoulder to calm him.

"There is one more thing—something I haven't told you
yet," she said to him. He looked at her with sudden concern.
"I need to speak to Red about what I plan to do," she explained.

"But Flæd," Edward protested, "he won't agree! He's so careful, and he's a Mercian!"

"He trusts me," Flæd said simply. "I need to ask him." Sulkily, Edward nodded, and shuffled reluctantly toward the doorway with Flæd. "Red," she said as she ducked around the curtain, "Edward and I have something to discuss. . . ."

The next day dawned chill and misty. Clouds covered the sun, which had warmed the pasture for so many summer days, and the river steamed in the unexpected coolness of the midsummer morning. At the starting point of the race Flæd stood beside her warder, grim-faced and hunched in the cold. For the first time in weeks she wore the grey cloak her mother had made for her, with the hood pulled over her hair and her hands wrapped in its warm folds.

As they had promised, Ethelred and the Mercian retainers who had come with him had been among the first to arrive at the racecourse that morning. Flæd could see Ethelred cantering his red warhorse to limber its legs as more people from the burgh gathered on foot and on horseback. Ethelred was calm, she could see, cooler than his horse, who toyed with the bit, trying to clamp it in his teeth and stretch into a longer run. Ethelred would have his hands full holding him back until the race began. She spotted a young sentry from her father's chambers (Dunstan was his name, she remembered) mounted on the yellow gelding from the pasture herd—a strong horse; the sentry had a chance. Other well-mounted men from the burgh came to mill about the starting point, riding among the Mercian visitors and eyeing the foreign riders and horses.

Through the mist Alfred and Ealhswith appeared, approaching the racecourse on foot. They stopped a little distance away from Flæd and her warder to survey the growing field of riders.

"Where is your brother?" the queen called out to Flæd. "Surely he is coming to see the race."

"I'm here, Mother," came Edward's voice. Wearing his own hooded cloak he rode up to them, perched high on Apple's withers. The grey horse had neither saddle nor bridle. Wulf trotted up behind, following them out of the murk.

"You will see more of the race from that tall seat," Alfred said to his son.

"I will see as much of it as I can," Edward replied. "I'm going to ride in it."

"Edward, these are all grown men," Ealhswith said anxiously, pointing to the riders grouped a little way off. "Many of them have ridden in battle, and their horses are used to the crowds of a charge. Your colt hasn't even a bridle to stop him if he runs away with you."

"He won't run away," Edward told her, patting his horse's dappled neck. "Red's been teaching him." Alfred motioned to Flæd's warder, and Flæd and Red came closer.

"Can my son ride in this race?" the king wanted to know.

"Your son has some skill," Red replied. "He sits the horse well." Beside him, Flæd twisted her hands more tightly in the wool of her cloak. Alfred looked at Edward and Apple with concern. The soft beat of approaching hooves made him turn in time to see Ethelred ease his tall red horse to a halt near them.

"The West Saxon royal family!" Ethelred shouted down with a smiling flash of his teeth. "Come to see a race on this fine summer morning!" He looked at Edward and his mount. "Your son rides in your stead," he asked Alfred, "on an unbridled horse?"

Alfred smiled. "You knew I would not ride against you again today," he said to his old friend, "but even I did not know until this morning that my son wished to ride for Wessex."

"It is good to see him in the race," Ethelred said heartily. His horse took several dancing steps toward Edward. "No saddle, either, boy? Mind your seat at the start," the aldorman advised him. He spoke to the king again. "I will not be able to watch for the safety of your child when we begin our run," he apologized, "but I will look for him after I have won the race." Ethelred gave Alfred and the queen another broad grin as he drew his reins across his horse's proud neck, turning the animal toward Flæd. "And I hope you will wait for me at the finish of the race, Lady," he said, leaning down toward her and speaking more softly, "for when I win, I will claim a kiss from my betrothed." With this, Ethelred brought his horse around and trotted back to the starting point.

"Yes, I will be waiting for you at the end of the race," Flæd said in a whisper, watching Ethelred's broad back disappear into the crowd. Briefly she met Edward's eyes, the two of them peering out at each other from beneath their sheltering hoods. Then Flæd slapped Apple's rump and sent Edward off toward the gathering of men and horses.

Ealhswith had hooked her fingers around Wulf's collar, and now the big dog was whining and pulling in the direction his master had gone. "We must follow them," the queen said to Alfred, "so you can give the sign to start, and so Wulf," she added breathlessly as the dog lunged again, "does not pull my arm from my body."

"Red and I would like to watch from there," Flæd told them, pointing to the place where the racecourse curved toward the river and a little clump of trees. The little herd of horses which had summered in the pasture was grouped in this place today. Flæd could see them grazing in the foggy air of the pasture, among them a lighter shape which she knew was Oat.

"You would rather watch from that far point?" her father asked, perplexed.

"To see the race midway," Red explained, his face impassive, "and to cheer Edward as he passes."

"Then we can hurry across the meadow to see the finish," Flæd added. Her father gave her a long look.

"As you wish," he said at last. "Join us as soon as you can." They separated. Edward's dog pulled Ealhswith along in jerks until Alfred took hold of the dog's collar instead. When they reached the crowded starting point, the king and queen found Bishop Asser and Father John among the group of retainers and royal guardsmen who had come to the field to watch.

"I have seen Edward mounted among the men," Asser said, "but where is Lady Æthelflæd?" Alfred told his advisor where Flæd and her warder had gone, and then passed the restless Wulf over to Father John, who tried to soothe him.

With one of his guards escorting him, Alfred walked briskly to the pole which had been pounded into the earth at the side of the racecourse to show the starting point. When the riders saw the king, they began to urge their horses forward into a series of lines, waiting for the king's signal. Near the front of the mass, Edward's grey mount and Ethelred's red warhorse jostled for position next to each other. The king raised his arm and the human voices silenced, leaving only the sound of horses' hooves and breath, and the jingle of their decorations. Then Alfred dropped his hand, the watching crowd shouted, and the riders surged forward.

Like the long curve of a scythe, the stream of horses cut through the mist and rounded the first bend of the racecourse, heading toward the river. Behind them loped a smaller grey shape, ears drawn flat and belly stretched out almost to the ground with each long stride. Wulf had escaped Father John's grasp.

It grew more difficult to see the racers as they passed close to the river and its thicker fog. Onlookers back at the starting point exclaimed and began to point as the herd of loose horses began to run with the others, riderless. For a moment the whole running pack passed behind a group of trees. When they emerged, closer now to the watching crowd, the free horses had dropped away, and Ethelred's red warhorse ran strongly in the lead.

All at once a dappled grey horse shot from the throng of riders and approached the front. It drew past Ethelred easily, and ran toward the excited voices of the people at the finish. Smoothly, the grey horse ran further and further ahead of the other riders, its own grey-hooded rider pressed flat along its neck. As it crossed the finish first, loud cheers rose up from the West Saxon viewers, and some who had noticed the king's son before the race shouted, "Edward! Edward!"

As the other riders pounded to the race's end, people on foot crowded around the grey-cloaked rider, who had moved a little way out into the pasture. There were exclamations over the absence of saddle or bridle on the horse. The pale horse stood patiently as many hands reached out to touch its flanks and to pat its rider's leather-shod foot. The mount seemed barely winded, while even Ethelred's big stallion hung his head, blowing hard just beyond the finish.

Pushing his way through the crowd, Ethelred met the king and queen as they made their way toward the winner.

"King Alfred," Ethelred said with a friendly cuff on his friend's shoulder, "I am very glad to see your boy well. I thought I saw his horse running without a rider as we passed the river." He fell into step with them. "One of my men already swears the race was bewitched—he says he saw a perfect twin of your son's mount running up to pass the grey horse, and then claims that a ghostly rider suddenly appeared on its back. The mist and too many cups of beer have dazed him this morning, I think."

"Or perhaps he is merely astonished that a boy could best these men, could best even you," Ealhswith said with a baffled look on her face. "I do not understand it myself."

"I wonder if I am beginning to understand," said Alfred, who had been looking across the meadow as they walked. Now he pointed to two human figures coming toward them through the hazy air. A third grey shadow skulked along at their heels.

"Ethelred's envoy, and Flæd, and Wulf!" Ealhswith said, squinting as the three shapes drew nearer. "Father John could not hold the dog when the horses began to run," she explained to Ethelred, "and the silly animal chased after his master."

"And found him, it seems," Alfred said strangely. He stopped, puting out a hand to halt the queen and the Mercian alderman. "Let us meet these three before we go to see the winner."

"Lady," Ethelred called out as the little group approached them, "you promised to greet me at the finish of the race!"

"Surely she was there before you," Alfred said softly as the cloaked figure pushed back the hood. Edward stood before them, a sheepish expression on his face. For a frozen moment Ethelred stared at the boy. Then the Mercian whirled, shouldering his way quickly into the crowd around the person on the grey horse. When he stood beside the rider, he shouted to be heard above the milling well-wishers.

"Lady," Ethelred blared, "show your face!" Atop the horse, the rider shook back the grey hood of the cloak. A long brown braid escaped the fabric. Flæd blinked down at the Mercian aldorman.

"I told you I would be waiting at the race's end," she said to him. A sudden hush took the crowd, and Flæd gripped the mane of her horse with bloodless fingers. Then Ethelred's laugh rang out over the gathered people. He held up his arms to her and lifted her to the ground as others in the crowd began to laugh with him, and some to cheer. Leading Flæd by the hand, he made his way back to the place where Alfred and his queen stood with Red and Edward.

"Trusted thane," Ethelred said to Red, "I have found your ward without her guardian. How is it that she left your protection?"

"She left me to ride with you," Red replied, with an almost imperceptible upturn of his lips. "That met our terms, I thought."

"But how was this done?" Ealhswith demanded. In response, Flæd put two fingers to her mouth and whistled out into the meadow. After a pause the sound of hoofbeats came to them through the foggy air, and Apple cantered up. He neighed to Oat, who was still surrounded by people, and his brother tossed his head and neighed back.

"Apple was Edward's mount," Flæd told them shyly. "He and Oat are a matched pair. I have a way of riding so no one can see me," she explained.

"But how did the two of you—how did Edward come to be with . . . ," the queen broke off, spreading her hands helplessly.

"Oat and I started the herd running," Flæd explained, "and I hung down on his side so we would look like just another loose horse. When the racers came around, Edward made Apple slow down" ("It wasn't easy," Edward mumbled) "and Oat and I rode on to take his place." Ethelred looked at Red.

"You have been teaching the king's daughter battle exercises?" the aldorman asked.

"I have, but she taught herself this, er, trick, and then showed me," Red replied. Ethelred was laughing again as he dropped to one knee in front of Flæd.

"Lady, I have misjudged my opponent—I am not usually so foolish." Flæd turned her face aside in embarrassment.

"I cheated in the race," she reminded him. "I am not often so deceptive." Saying this, she caught Red's eye, and blushed at certain memories.

"Indeed, you cannot be named the winner if you did not run the whole race," Ethelred said thoughtfully as he got to his feet. "In that case, I claim my winner's kiss," he said, and did.

When Ethelred and his men left late that morning, Flæd stood with her warder on the burgh wall and watched them go. The aldorman noticed me, Flæd thought, I made him notice me. And the kiss, she remembered, that quick, hard pressure of his mouth on hers. Flæd knew little of such things, but she did not think that had been the sort of kiss a lover would give. Ethelred had laughed in surprise and pleasure at her trick. He had intended to tease her with the kiss, but instead it had become a salute from an opponent to the victor.

Did she like him? I don't know yet, Flæd decided warily. Perhaps now, at least, Ethelred had learned to think of her as something more than his king's quiet daughter. Standing on the wall, Flæd tried to pick out Ethelred's dwindling shape among the Mercian party. She thought of the length of Ethelred's arms reaching up to take her down from her horse. She recalled the width of his chest and the measure of his leg as he reclined comfortably in his chair at the feast. She remembered the height of his shoulder—just above her line of sight. As the band of retainers and their lord splashed into the river at the ford, she turned away and hurried down the stairs, heading for the forge. There was just enough time for the smith to fit a fine suit of ring mail to Ethelred's size before she left to join him in Mercia.

The Trap

ETHELRED RAN A HAND ALONG HIS HORSE'S LEGS, LIFTING EACH foot in turn to check the hooves. It had been unwise to ride the animal so hard just before they began the journey home, but Alfred always made him act like a boy. Ethelred had led his party more slowly coming back, and now at twilight they were halfway home. No lame horses yet, he thought, patting his mount's shoulder. The big red horse had been a good battle companion in past years. Ethelred didn't want a foolish race to ruin him now.

"Press on, or make camp?" he turned to ask his second in command, who was attending to his own horse.

"She could go farther"—the thane rubbed his mare's bony face—"but what about the others?" Ethelred looked around at his company. It had been extravagant to bring twenty men on this peaceful visit, but he had wanted to show that Mercia was strong and prosperous—a worthy home for the daughter of Alfred the Great. And he was glad now that he had done it. Alfred had been pleased to see him riding in strength, he thought. And Æthelflæd . . . well, the girl had been more interesting than he had expected.

Prudence was best, Ethelred decided. Why not arrive in Lunden a bit later the next day, after a full night's sleep for men and horses? There was no obvious need to return sooner.

"Tell them we'll stay here for the night," he instructed his retainer. The men began unsaddling their horses, unpacking food and blankets. Someone started a fire.

There was no warning before the attack. The raiders had come up around them so close that five men went down before Ethelred had time to reach for his sword. The next moments were desperate—cries and clangs, the crashing bulk of loose and terrified horses. A skirmish moved through the fire, and coals scattered into the dry grass, which blazed up here and there at the edges of the battle. Ethelred was slashed across his shield arm, but his retainers closed in beside him and fought body against body.

Suddenly it was over. The Mercians in their defensive knot hesitated as the attackers broke off and retreated out into the darkness, and when at last they shouted their battle cries and gave chase, every enemy had vanished.

Clutching his arm, the chief alderman called out for a torch, and went to see to his fallen men. Seven were dead, and five more wounded, though none so badly that he could not travel. Ethelred crouched down beside the youngest of the slain men—a boy, really, whose father had asked the aldorman to let him come for a view of the land. What had the raiders wanted, to make them strike down a few noblemen and then run, Ethelred wondered wrathfully. He shook his head. Only one thing was certain. A message must go to Alfred tonight to prevent Lady Æthelflæd's journey. Heaving himself to his feet, Ethelred went to find Cenwulf.

On the wooded high ground overlooking the shattered camp, the leader of the raiding party stood, watching the members of Ethelred's party tend to their wounded and gather their dead. Beside him stood a short, dirty man, who was also his most talented archer. There had always been a chance that the assassination of the chief aldorman might fail—the thanes of the Mercian court were seasoned fighters. But a greater prize was coming, and the only real difficulty was the messenger Ethelred would surely send.

A movement at the edge of the camp caught his eye, and he gripped the shoulder of the man waiting next to him. There, he pointed to a single horseman picking his way along the river toward them. The messenger would soon be within their range, and beyond earshot of his companions.

One arrow brought down the man. A second dropped his horse. The man on the hillside smiled. In a few days he would meet Æthelflæd of Wessex again.

IV
Summer's End

19

Leaving Home

"WATCH," EALHSWITH WHISPERED TO HER DAUGHTER AS THEY stood beside the wagon. The queen glanced around to be sure that no one else was looking. From the folds of her dress, she produced the flat box which held Ethelred's golden betrothal gifts. Swiftly she slipped it into a little hollow beneath the seat Flæd would occupy on the long ride. The box fit securely, and was almost impossible to notice in the dark cranny. Flæd nodded to show that she would remember the secret place. She had slept little, and her throat felt thick with the unhappiness of this day.

In the week since Ethelred's departure, neither Flæd's final lessons with her tutor nor the sessions with Red which concluded her training had kept her mind from the fact that she must truly leave her home. Ever since Flæd had learned of her own betrothal, something in her had hoped that her family might come with her to Mercia to attend the marriage ceremony. Their company on the journey would not change the fact that she was leaving them, of course, but it might have eased the separation a little. Attending the talks in her father's chamber, however, had convinced Flæd that the family would not leave the burgh at this season. Uncertainties at the border required the king's presence here with his main advisors. And the unwieldy number of guards and servants required to move the entire royal household would make the excursion slow, and even dangerous, for her mother and the other children. It would be best if Flæd went to Mercia alone, and quickly, with a smaller guard.

Flæd knew that these last few days and nights in the burgh were a gift from her father. He could have sent her with Ethelred, as the Mercian aldorman himself had suggested. Yet she could muster little gratitude. She could hardly bring herself to reply to the king as he explained the arrangements for her journey. Ten retainers for her guard, and Red, too, of course—yes, she had nodded to show that she would feel secure with that number of men. Two wagons for her dowry goods. They would like her to sit with the driver of the lead wagon. Would she agree to this? *I can ride,* Flæd remembered saying to Ethelred in the great hall, and she had shown them all that she could. But even her father seemed to believe that she would be safest if she were neatly packed with the other gifts bound for Mercia. With a limp shrug, Flæd had agreed to this request, as well.

Now on the morning of her journey, Flæd stood beside her mother and stared miserably at the bustle of activity around her. Outside the storehouse serving men were load-

ing the last items—heavy chests filled with silver coins—
into the wagons which would travel to Mercia with the
king's daughter. As the servants finished their work, Ealhswith took Flæd's hand, and the two of them walked away
from the well-guarded dowry. Red, who had helped to load
the silver, followed a little way behind.

Through the fresh morning air Flæd and her mother
crossed the burgh, heading toward the king's council chamber. Ealhswith's calm voice continued with the list of things
packed in the wagons, and Flæd kept nodding, hardly hearing, until she noticed that her mother had fallen silent. The
queen halted and looked at her daughter. She stretched out
a hand to finger Flæd's neat braid.

"You are the first of our children to leave us," Ealhswith
murmured. Reaching into the leather pocket hanging from
her belt, the queen drew out her ivory comb carved with sea
animals. "You loved this as a child," Ealhswith said. "It will
help you remember your time in your father's burgh, and
perhaps your own child will love it someday." With a hard,
quick embrace, the queen sent Flæd on her way. "I'll come to
see you off," she told her. "Now your father wishes to speak
with you."

In Alfred's chambers Flæd found her father, Asser, and
Father John gathered at the council table, just as she had
seen them on so many spring and summer nights.

"Come sit with us," her father invited. Flæd found a stool
and pulled it up to the table. "We have something for you."

The king motioned to John, who drew out a well-bound little book and passed it across the table. Flæd picked it up, feeling the soft leather against her palm.

"A handbook," she said, looking at her father, "like yours."

"Open it," Alfred suggested. Flæd lifted the cover. On the vellum of the first page bold capitals proclaimed KING ALFRED COMMANDED THAT I SHOULD BE MADE. Flæd turned to the next page and caught her breath. There before her, sewn into the new little volume, lay the opening leaf that Alfred had shown her in his own handbook so many nights before. Amid its maze of gold and color, the letter *æsc* shone out boldly. Tears filled Flæd's eyes as she looked up at her father.

"You took it from your mother's book," she said, "the *æsc* from the book you won."

"From the book I 'learned,' " Alfred agreed. "But you have earned your handbook with better scholarship than mine. We thought you should have a place to copy favorite passages, just as I have done in my later years. So look, we have started the collection for you. I have given you this initial—the one which begins both of our names—to remind you of the beginnings of your family's learning."

"Turn to the next page," Bishop Asser advised her. "Father John and I have chosen a maxim for you from the great book of poetry. I do not think you have seen it before."

Flæd delicately leafed past the illuminated page, and on

the next newly ruled sheet she read, "A woman must shine, cherished among her people. She must be open-hearted and generous with horses and treasure. With honor she must offer the cup to her lord's hand. She must know what is wise for both of them as rulers in the hall."

"They will cherish you in Mercia," Father John said, "as we have cherished you here with us. Rule well with Ethelred, Lady Æthelflæd." Flæd looked down at the maxim once more. It had been copied out in Father John's perfect hand.

Flæd still clutched the little book as she stood at the gate of the burgh in her travelling clothes, waiting for the wagons. The ten retainers who would travel with her had gathered on their horses. Red had joined them, reining his own horse close to the youngest of the retainers in the mounted guard. It was the sentry Dunstan, Flæd saw, the young man who had raced the yellow gelding against Ethelred last week. Flæd saw Red lean toward Dunstan to say something. She remembered hearing that the young sentry had finished the race just after Ethelred himself—he had become something of a hero for keeping his plain West Saxon mount so close upon the heels of Ethelred's fine warhorse. It was good to have him in her party, Flæd decided forlornly. It was good to have at least two familiar faces—his and Red's—in the group.

A flurry of movement caught Flæd's eye, and she looked back toward the burgh to find her little sisters running ahead of their attendants. Dove charged headlong into Flæd and clung to her clothes, catching her breath.

"We brought you something," Ælf panted, right behind Dove. "We don't know whether in Mercia they have the same flowers and things that grow here."

"We want to make flower crowns and stick horses with you when we come to Lunden," Dove explained, "so we gathered some seeds just in case." The two sisters held out a cloth bundle. "Be careful," Dove warned. Flæd sat down on the ground and sheltered the little package in her lap. She untied the corners of the cloth and looked down at a jumble of seedpods and two ripe bulrush heads. In the center of the collection lay a slender length of willow.

"The willow wand will grow if you plant it in the ground and give it water," Ælf promised her. "The Grey Man told us it would." Ælf glanced anxiously at Red, who had dismounted and now stood back against the wall, holding the reins of his horse. He nodded to assure her it was so.

Flæd hugged the little girls together. "I will find a place to grow all of these," she told her sisters, "and I will show them to you when you come to see me."

Gathering the little bundle together again, she stood, and saw that her mother and father had arrived at the gate while she talked with Dove and Ælf. Ealhswith had brought little Æthelweard with her, and he clung to his mother's finger as the queen and Flæd held each other. Flæd knelt down to say good-bye to the small brother who would scarcely remember her after she had gone. "Flæd," he said, pointing at her face, and laughing when she poked his round belly through the little shift he wore. "Horse," he said, spotting something more interesting than his sister, and tugging his mother toward the mounted retainers around the gate.

But her other brother did not appear. With an ache Flæd wondered if things had really changed so much between her and Edward. Before her betrothal Edward had always come to see her off, even if she were leaving the burgh for less than a day to visit a nearby monastery or farmstead. And now, on the morning when she would leave the burgh forever, he had not come. It was true that they had spent far less time together this summer than in the past. Busy in the council room or training with Red, Flæd had sensed that she and Edward were growing apart without knowing what to do about it. Still, I thought he would be here today, she mourned, I thought he would want to say good-bye.

Suddenly Flæd felt hopeless. Edward, a person she still counted on, had deserted her. She was already lonely, and she had yet to face the crowd of unfamiliar faces waiting for her in Mercia. Ethelred's face would be the only one she would recognize among those strangers, and although she knew his features, she still knew very little of the man behind them.

"Where is Edward?" she asked her father.

Alfred frowned. "We could not find him," he said. "I

thought he might be with you already." Seeing Flæd's disappointment, he clasped her hand in his warm fingers. "Edward will visit you in Mercia," he said. "He will want to."

The king pointed toward the burgh to show her that the wagons were coming. "I have decided to send two friends with you to Lunden," he said. "I think they will help you miss your home a little less." In the harness of the lead wagon trotted Apple and Oat, groomed and shod for the journey. The wagon stopped in front of Flæd, and Oat, the near horse, leaned over to nibble at her tunic, looking for the pocket of sweets he remembered.

"Thank you," Flæd choked, looking at Alfred as she pressed her cheek against the horse's warm neck. So this was why her two greys had stayed unclaimed in the pasture all summer—the king had intended them for his daughter's journey to Mercia. Flæd turned to embrace her father, fiercely, one last time. Then she climbed to her seat beside the driver, and Red moved into place beside her wagon on his horse. Today her warder wore a mail shirt over his leather tunic. A heavy iron helm covered the leather cap on his head.

"Farewell, Envoy of Ethelred," Alfred called to him. "Bring my daughter safely to your aldorman." Red bowed. At a signal from Alfred, the drivers spoke to their horses, and the wagons lurched forward with a creak of wooden wheels, bumping along until they fell into the ruts of the road.

"Wait!" came a shout behind them. At a run, Edward appeared behind the wagons, and came up level with them as they stopped. Red-faced and panting, he stood, bent double, with his hands on his knees. "I . . . was in the scriptorium," he said between breaths, ". . . almost . . . missed you." Edward straightened and held up a small, flat leather pouch to his sister. "Open it on the way," he breathed, and then stepped back from the wagon. Flæd tried to scramble down from her seat, but the driver stopped her with a gentle hand.

"We've got a long way to go before nightfall," he told her. "We can't wait." Flæd looked at Red, whose restless eyes had stilled for a moment as he looked at Edward.

"A moment, Lady. Then we have to go." He shook his head apologetically, turning back to his uneasy survey of the terrain ahead. Flæd slid down and stood before Edward. She would have thrown herself toward him, she was so relieved to see him, but he would not look at her. Flæd searched for something to say.

"We . . . we never read any other poems together," she said. Edward wrinkled his face, surprised at the words, then shrugged, head still down. "Well, it's your turn," Flæd announced abruptly as an idea resolved itself. Edward raised his eyes, confused. "It's your turn to take the great book and read it when Father John isn't looking. When you come to Mercia, I will expect you to tell me a new story from it." She made her face severe. "I will send you straight home if you don't." A trace of a smile showed on Edward's mouth for a moment, then disappeared.

"Your companions can't wait," he echoed the driver.

Heavily she nodded, and turned back to the wagon. With ginger hands and feet, she climbed the wheel spokes to reach her seat, then turned to look at Edward once more. As the driver gave the command to move forward again, Wulf trotted up to sit beside Edward, and before the dust rose up to block her view, Flæd saw her brother raise his hand in farewell.

Edward's gift lay untouched on Flæd's seat as they travelled that morning along the course of the river, skirting low wooded hills. She watched, empty-eyed, as they passed between fields where yellow stubble stood sharply in the bare ground. Farmers tended little fires here and there, and Flæd tasted the bitter smoke as the wagons rumbled by.

Ethelred. She was going to see him—no, to live with him, to be his *wife*. This past week she had forced herself to look at her mother and see not the woman who protected and loved three daughters and two sons, but the queen whose life and body were bound to Alfred, King of Wessex. This meant more than sitting beside the king in the great hall, and bearing the king's cup for his retainers to drink, Flæd had begun to acknowledge. Life and body, Flæd thought, trying to understand it. It means to share his bed, to bear him children, to know the thoughts he shares with you. Saint Juliana fought, even martyred herself, when her father tried to give her to a heathen husband, the girl found herself remembering. I always thought Juliana did it because of faith, Flæd grimaced, but maybe it was fear. Ethelred was no heathen, but when she thought of being his, her body and her life being his, she was afraid.

It had become a bright, cool day, and when the sun had moved high in the sky, Flæd finally turned her dreary face away from the countryside and took up the pouch Edward had given her. It was so light it felt empty, but when Flæd looked inside she found a single folded sheet of vellum. Carefully she spread the page out on her lap. In blotted, slightly smudged writing she found the following message:

Greetings Flæd. Father John has been teaching me to use a reed pen and ink. This is my first message, and I am sorry about the blots. Father John says I may have vellum to write to you whenever there is a rider going to Mercia. You could send a message back in my leather pouch to keep it safe. This writing has taken a long time. Wulf and I will run to bring it to you. Send a message back to me soon. Edward.

The letters grew more blurred beneath Flæd's gaze, and she quickly folded the note and put it away. Edward had not forsaken her, but for now the thought did not make her feel any better about leaving home.

That night Flæd sat next to Red, staring into the little fire they had made at the center of their camp. Around them the retainers and drivers were settling down for the night. The horses were picketed at the edges of the camp, or tied to the wagons which had been drawn up a short distance from the fire. Flæd was remembering the smearing of Edward's uneven script—the ink had not yet dried when Edward hurried to fold his message. She thought of her brother running after her with his first letter, and then of the gifts from her father and mother and sisters. Clenching her jaw, she pushed back the sadness she could feel welling up. She turned to Red.

"Tell me what Mercia is like, so I will know it when we get there."

Red poked at the fire with a charred stick. "We came into Mercia before sunset," he told her.

Flæd looked around her, surprised enough to forget her grieving for a moment. "This is Mercia?" They had gone a little way from the river to make their camp, but had she not known better, Flæd could easily have imagined that they were in the woods just outside her own burgh. "How is Mercia different from Wessex?" she demanded.

"They're not so different," Red admitted. "Even their greatest kings have been like each other." He reached into a pouch on his belt and drew out a single silver coin. He held it out for Flæd to take. "There is your father's image. That writing on the edge names him *Rex Anglorum*—King of the English People."

"It does," Flæd agreed, fingering the letters.

"Another king held that title, and marked it on his money, long before your father's father's birth," Red said.

"Offa, King of Mercia, *Rex Anglorum*. Offa overcame the Danes, made law among Mercians and Saxons, even conferred with Charlemagne." Red dropped his stick into the fire. "This will help you understand Mercians." He settled back against the pile of gear behind him. "Our name, *mierce*, means 'boundary folk.' Alfred is king of English Mercia now, so we don't hold our borders against him. But like Offa, we keep our borders strong against the Danes, the Welsh—anyone who would be our enemy. Alfred trusts Ethelred to do this."

Feeling the nervous discomfort that always accompanied her thoughts of Ethelred, Flæd remembered the man's heated discussion of the threat at his western border. Mercians were boundary folk, Red said. She began to understand Ethelred's passionate talk in the council chamber.

Flæd looked up at the clear sky, thinking of the rainy night when she and Red had sat, like this, by a little fire. He had spoken easily to her that evening. Would he be open to her queries again, she wondered.

"Is Ethelred . . . a good man?" She brought out the words with difficulty. Red threw a bit of bark into the fire.

"After Burgred," he said, "I didn't think I'd trust another man to lead me." He snapped another piece of bark between his fingers, then turned to look directly at her. "When they brought me back to Mercia, they took me to see the aldorman. He said"—Red swallowed, shifting his gaze—"Ethelred said he would keep looking for my girls, and he has. He is a good man." There was a pause as the two of them looked silently into the fire again.

"I told you once that I used to listen to poetry in the great hall, in the time when I was proud to be Burgred's hearth-companion," Red said unexpectedly. Flæd sat up straighter to listen. "One night the king asked the man who entertained us to recite a few maxims, like the ones your own father loves." Flæd bobbed her head in recognition, remembering the little handbook with its words about the duty of a woman. "One of the maxims the poet chose I have never forgotten," Red went on. "The man said, 'The shield must be at the ready, the javelin on its shaft, the edge on the sword, and a point on the spear.'

"Those were not the most beautiful of verses," her warder acknowledged with a twitch of his mouth, "but they said something I believe is true. All these things we use—the shield, the spear, the sword—belong in their proper places, sharpened or made strong, ready when we need them. That night I thought, 'I am the edge on Burgred's sword.' I felt ready in my place, like a polished weapon, set to strike where my lord wished."

"But then he wronged you," Flæd said quietly.

"Yes, and that changed nothing," Red returned, startling her with the intensity of his voice. "I became Ethelred's trusted man, the edge on *his* sword, still ready in my place when I was needed." Red turned to face her again. "If someone makes a choice for us, and we don't like it—maybe we even hate it—it's still our duty to keep ourselves sharp, or strong, to make ourselves ready for whatever task comes to us."

The edge on the sword. To stay sharp and strong, ready in one's place in spite of trouble. Her warder could see that she was afraid, Flæd knew, and he was trying to help.

Red glanced around them with the wariness he had shown all day. "It will be better," he said, almost speaking to himself now, "when you are safe in Lunden with Ethelred." Something in his tone told Flæd that he was thinking of a threat more ominous than her dejected spirits.

"Is there still danger from the Welsh front?" Flæd asked in a low voice.

Red sighed. "No new sign of trouble," he answered, "but Danes don't give up so easily, nor do Welshmen." For a moment he prodded the fire, which was burning down to red coals. The he reached into the pile behind him and pulled out a heavy cloth sack.

"I have something for you," he said to Flæd. "Didn't know when to give it." Red untied the mouth of the sack and drew out the mail shirt Flæd had worn in practice. He brought out a leather cap set with plates of metal, and a belt to go around the mail shirt which held a dagger in a plain leather sheath. "There's a shield for you in the second wagon, and a light sword," he said, "in case you need them."

Flæd felt the weight of the mail shirt across her legs where Red had draped it. She drew the dagger from its sheath and tested its edge against her thumb. A hairline of blood appeared where she had touched the blade.

"You think there might be an attack," she said, a chill running through her.

"I promised that you would reach Mercia safely," her warder said, returning the things to the sack and placing the bundle beside her. He had done his best to ensure that she and all those with her were prepared for surprises, Flæd realized. Because Red had requested it, their party of ten retainers in addition to herself and Red was half the size of the one Ethelred had brought to their burgh—her escort travelled quick and light. Yet there were still enough fighting men to mount a defense, in spite of the fact that the king's other advisors had not anticipated trouble on the journey.

Red got to his feet and retrieved his sword. "I have the first watch," he said brusquely. "Sleep well, Lady." She lay back, watching him adjust his armor and check his weapons. Safe, she thought, turning onto her side and closing her eyes, I'm safe with him.

Red's feet made the softest of sounds crossing the flattened grass of their campsite. As he passed her, he bent down to touch her hair with his callused hand.

20

Blood Money

THE SOUND OF BOOTED FEET RUNNING TOWARD HER WOKE HER
before she heard the scream.

"Quiet, Lady," Red's voice whispered tensely into her ear
as he pulled her to a sitting position in the dark and dragged
the mail shirt over her head. "Come with me." Thrusting
the helmet and dagger into her hands, he propelled her toward the wagons. Flæd heard another scream. The noise was
not human, her racing mind told her. The horses on the outskirts of the camp were making the awful sounds.

As they reached the first wagon, Red grabbed his own
dagger from his belt and slashed the tethers which bound
Oat and Apple there. With one hand he snatched at the short
strap still hanging from Apple's halter, and with the other he
gripped Flæd's arm, pulling her closer.

"Raiders," he hissed. "They're coming in a half-circle"—
he indicated the sweep of the attack with a gesture from the
north to the south edges of their camp—"moving down the
hill. Get out"—he boosted her silently onto Apple's back—

"and don't let them see you. Watch the camp from the grove we passed at sunset. If strangers ride out, don't come back. Go east when you can, along the river on to Lunden. A hard ride will bring you there in half a day." For a paralyzed moment Flæd stared down at her warder. "Go now!" he insisted, jabbing her horse in the ribs.

Apple surged forward, and Oat wheeled to run with him. With her head lowered among the blowing strands of Apple's mane, Flæd clung to the grey horse, heading for the thicket Red had ordered her to reach. Ahead of her in the darkness she could see a large black shape on the ground. The shape heaved, and another dreadful scream cut through the night. Horror-stricken, Flæd realized that she was looking at one of the camp's horses lying at the end of its picket, its hamstrings sliced through. Nearby she could see the shadows of two men closing in on another horse as the animal jerked at its rope in terror. Almost without thinking Flæd wound her fingers tightly in Apple's knotted mane and slipped down, hanging on the side of her galloping horse farthest from the figures she had seen. She heard shouts in a strange language, heard the sound of men running behind her mount, and then felt her horse swerve as a rock thudded into his side. Several other rocks struck the ground around the two running horses, then nothing more.

Flæd's arms and abdominal muscles were burning. She would have to release her grip or regain her seat in the next few strides. Biting back a groan, she pulled her torso over the horse's back and swung a leg across. The men had disappeared behind them, and as she urged Apple to even greater speed, Flæd realized that they had been chasing her two horses out of camp, not trying to catch them. She had not been seen.

Red had told her to take cover, and crouched over Apple's neck, Flæd could think of nothing she wanted more than a place to hide. But another idea was growing painfully inside her. He trained me, her mind repeated again and again, he trained me to fight. Through her fear she remembered days in the pasture, the balance and counterbalance of weapons, Red's quiet voice, her muscles growing stronger. She should follow her guardian's orders, shouldn't she? Red had prepared and sharpened her for combat—this thought rose through her fear as the shouts of the battle rose through the night—but he had insisted that she flee this battle.

Veering onto the road with a sob of frustration, Flæd kicked Apple into a hard gallop away from the fighting. Looking back over her shoulder toward the camp, she could see the distant shapes of men struggling with each other, and somehow she could not feel relief at leaving them behind. Then her stomach gave a lurch—someone was running away from the camp toward her. No, the figure was not heading directly along her path, she saw with another turn of her head. He appeared to have picked up a trail leading through the bracken. It looked like his course would take him into the trees north of the fighting.

Possibilities flashed through Flæd's head. This was almost certainly not a member of the West Saxon party. A deserter from among the raiders? He was more likely to be a messenger, she thought, sent to bring back more attackers. Red could not be aware of anyone leaving the battle—he was still back in the thick of the fight. . . .

A stab of anger pierced Flæd's fear. Someone had been sent to bring fresh warriors down upon her outnumbered band. More violence against their peaceful party—against her companions! And she had been sent away, commanded only to save herself. She would not do it. With a plunging turn she brought Apple around and urged her horse after the running man. Maybe on horseback with her dagger, she thought as she grasped its hilt with shaking fingers, she could stop him.

Flæd and Apple came to the place where the man's little track left the main road, and Flæd pushed her horse to keep their speed along the narrow way. Soon trees were whipping against her arms and Apple's sides, and the runner had come into view again. Flæd and her mount lunged forward. She was gaining on the running man, and at last he noticed her. But now Flæd had come very close. Dagger in hand, she leaned over to swipe at him just as Red had taught her to do with the practice sword. The man whirled around, ducking beneath Flæd's stroke. His fingers dug into her leg, pulling her and her mount off balance. She lost her seat and tumbled sideways, striking the ground hard with one shoulder before Apple's heavy body crashed down after her. A flailing hoof clipped her chin, and with an awful jerk she found stillness, blackness.

Flæd opened her eyes and saw the moon shining down on her through fronds of bracken. Near her ear a horse blew softly through its nose, and she heard the sound of big teeth cropping grass. She tried to roll over and gasped at the pain she felt in her neck and jaw. With a moan she sat up. Oat and Apple were grazing at the edge of the path a stone's throw away from her. Shakily she stood and took several steps before she stumbled over something on the ground.

A body lay in front of her. Flæd scrambled backward in fright, but the figure did not move, and slowly she crept forward again to take another look. In the moonlight she recognized the face of the runner she had tried to stop, and she could see that his neck was broken. Around him the ground cover was flattened, the earth churned by hooves. Flæd guessed that the man had been caught beneath her falling horse.

Could she have brought herself to kill him with her knife if she had been given the chance? She had aimed a blow at him from horseback, she remembered as she backed away and struggled to her feet, stomach churning. To kill a man—that was what her training had taught her. But she had never actually tried it before.

The horses snorted nervously as she limped up, but Flæd caught their halters and spoke in a low voice to calm them.

When they quieted, she stripped off her belt and sawed it into two leather thongs, which she looped through each horse's halter. Cautiously she led the pair a few lengths further into the bracken, until they reached a little thicket where she snubbed their heads up close to the trunk of a tree. She left them there and crept back to the edge of the road.

Another rider was coming. Still gripping her dagger, Flæd crouched down, watching the figure on the road draw closer. She shifted the knife in her hand, finding a better grip. The rider's face was still in shadow, but now on the horse's bridle and saddle she could see the strange shapes of unfamiliar decorations. This was not a mount she knew. Silently Flæd edged to one side as the rider reined up at the site of her fall. The person dismounted with a creaking of leather and ring mail, peering out at the broken undergrowth.

Then Flæd was behind him, pricking her knife into the back of his neck. She shook with the horror of what she thought she would have to do. The man was suddenly very still. "Lady?" she heard him whisper as he stood there rigidly. "Is that the lady Æthelflæd?"

"Who are you?" she whispered with swollen lips, bracing her arm for the thrust.

"It's Dunstan, Lady, Dunstan from your father's burgh. The envoy from Mercia—Red—he sent me to find you."

"Red sent you?" Flæd asked, stepping around the man and looking at his face for the first time. She recognized the young retainer—it *was* Dunstan, just as he had claimed.

"Where is my warder? What happened at the camp?" she demanded, pain throbbing through her face with every word.

"Lady, he is badly injured," Dunstan said. "We have taken this raiding party, but there may be others. He sent me on this captured horse. . . ." Flæd was already crashing through the brush toward her horses. "Lady!" he cried as she plunged out of the thicket on Apple's back, Oat close beside them, "Lady Æthelflæd, wait!"

Flæd hardly recognized the camp as she galloped through its outskirts past the bodies of horses who now lay silent and unmoving. The bundles of possessions where men had bedded down for the night were strewn everywhere. Torn cloth, shattered boxes, and broken earthenware pots and cups littered the ground. Flæd headed toward the wagons and the center of camp where a fire still burned. One of the wagons had been tipped on its side. Sacks of grain had been ripped apart, their contents spilling out onto the ground. Two of the boxes of silver lay smashed in a wagon bed, surrounded by a sea of coins. Flæd slid down from Apple's back and ran toward the campfire, where she could see men moving around several prone forms.

"Where's Red? Where is he?" she said frantically as she burst into the firelit circle.

"Lady Æthelflæd!" said one man, running to catch at her hand. "You are unharmed? Your face . . ."

"Where is Red?" Flæd said in a whisper that felt like a shriek. Dread filled her as she saw the man hesitate.

"He is here," the man said at last, "on the other side of the fire." Encircling her shoulders with his arm, he led her around the flames. There on the ground lay Red, his face gaunt in the flickering shadows. Blood soaked his short hair, and the leather cap which had been removed and placed beside him showed a great tear on one side. Flæd knelt down and reached for her warder's hand. She felt a strange stiffness in his fingers. She touched his cheek. Even close to the warmth of the fire, it was growing cold.

"Lady," said a soft voice. The man who had brought her to Red crouched down, and Flæd recognized him as one of the wagon drivers. "I know some healing," he told her, "but the wound was too bad." Quietly he began to tell her what had happened. "The envoy saw the raiders first, and made the rest of us circle behind while they were maiming the horses. He hid in camp. When they found the wagons they tore them apart, looking for something, and all of a sudden he rose up and ran at them alone. He killed three before they cut him down." The man bowed his head in grief. "We were running to join him, just as he had planned. We surprised them from behind and killed five more before the rest put down their weapons. We bound up the prisoners, Lady."

Flæd could not speak. Her hand still rested on Red's unmoving chest. *He killed three before they cut him down ... the wound was too bad.* She felt a terrible wrench as she remembered how often she had wished that his constant watching would end, and that he would leave her. No, her mind keened, no, no. My protector, she squeezed her eyes shut. My friend. With a great effort she looked back at the man who had shown her the body.

"Are any others dead from our party?"

The driver shook his head. "No, but the raiders destroyed all of our horses," he added. "None of us was meant to escape alive."

Gently, Flæd placed her warder's big hand back on the ground beside him. On the firelit ground nearby lay a trampled blanket. She shook the dust and leaves from it and spread it over Red's body, folding the cloth back neatly at his shoulders. "He is cold," she faltered, not looking at her companion.

Flæd stood and limped back toward the wagons. Some of her father's retainers sat exhausted in little clusters. Others tended wounds, and one or two had returned to the wagons to begin salvaging what goods they could, scooping the spilled coins into empty grain sacks. She stopped beside the seat at the front of the wagon where she had sat the day before. Far back in the little space her mother had shown her, the box with Ethelred's gifts lay undisturbed.

"Lady!" a young man's voice cried, and Dunstan came hurrying up. "The envoy charged me with your care, and I . . ." Flæd turned away from him, fighting back the anguish that crossed her face. She could not let the thought of Red silent on the ground overwhelm her now, she tried to remind herself. She knew that their little party must regroup—how should this be done? Someone among these men would know what to do. Someone would tell her how they should go forward from this evil place.

"Please gather our men," she said shakily. In a few moments the little travelling party had collected before her. Two retainers had blood on their clothes from wounds, and one driver showed a messy gash under one eye.

"Are you well enough to continue?" Flæd asked him. The man nodded. Flæd searched the faces of the other men, looking for the one prepared to lead them. Some did not look back at her, peering nervously out into the night instead. Two younger thanes met her eye eagerly, but she shied away from their gaze. *I'm not the one*, she rejected the thought. *One of these experienced fighters is the man you want.* All of them were waiting to see what she would say. In a small voice she addressed the retainers. "How many prisoners have we taken?"

"Five, my lady," one of them answered, "and eight raiders are dead."

"There is one other, back along the road. I . . . I think it would be right to bury them," Flæd said.

"My lady," said another man, stepping forward, "I know some of the prisoners' speech, and they have spoken to me. They plead for their lives, and offer wergild in exchange for the life of the man they killed." Wergild was legal payment for a freeman's death—a fixed sum of money in exchange for a life. The retainer's face hardened with anger. "They say that although he was clearly of common birth, he fought well. They offer two times the value of a churl." A murderous silence gripped the little circle of men, and Flæd felt a flash of rage and sorrow like a hot sword in her chest. For several seconds she said nothing. Then, in an icy tone, she began to issue orders.

"Have the prisoners bury their own dead. Give them water, and make a place for them in one of the wagons. They will come with us to Lunden."

"To Lunden, Lady?" It was the same retainer again—the one who had spoken to the prisoners. "Surely we must go back to the king's burgh after this disaster! Some of us have travelled in this country, but none of our party can guide us like the Mercian envoy. He knew the fastest way to Lunden, and he would have known where we could best defend ourselves from more raiders. Now who will save us if they come again?"

Flæd looked at the man's frightened, querulous expression. This was not the leader she had hoped for. Would no other thane come forward?

"Red told me we are half a day's hard ride east of Lunden," she said warily. "We have come more than half the distance of our journey. Do we not face as much danger in going back as we do in going forward?"

"We should go back," the dissenting retainer insisted, raising his voice. "We should return home."

Flæd tried to think. If their party reached the burgh, Alfred would surely muster a small army to escort her back to Lunden. But there was still every chance that they would be pursued on their retreat, and no West Saxons from the king's burgh would be watching for their arrival, ready to come to their aid. Lunden was somewhere not far ahead of them—Red had thought that she could find it on her own, if she needed to. He had been trying to train me to protect myself, to do his job in case I ever found myself without him, Flæd remembered.

"I believe Red would have wanted us to travel on to Lunden," she said out loud. "Does anyone agree?" Silence settled over the men again, broken only by the crackling of the fire.

"We do," said one of the young thanes at last, speaking for himself and his companion. "We will come with you."

"And I," said Dunstan, stepping forward to stand beside her. "I made a promise to the envoy." That's right, Flæd thought with a little sinking feeling, Red sent someone to help me. He wasn't really sure I could take care of myself.

"Foolishness," the angry thane resisted. "We are too small already. Our company should stay together."

"We should," agreed a stocky, broad-shouldered man with a bandaged leg. He limped to join the retainers clustered around Flæd, and one by one, the seven remaining men followed. Flæd looked at the scowling man who stood alone opposite her.

"Please," she said, "we need your sword, your skill with the prisoners' language. Our company is small," she echoed his plea, "we should stay together." Slowly the man uncurled his fists. Stone-faced, he nodded.

Still no one else spoke, and Flæd wondered futilely who would tell her what she ought to do next. Finally she looked to the two drivers. "Find as many of the raiders' horses as you can," she told them. "We will need mounts and teams by daybreak." Flæd stepped back and spoke to all of the men again. "Ethelred must be told of this attack. Perhaps you can decide among you who should ride ahead to Lunden. The rest of us must be ready to ride at dawn."

Flæd ignored the murmur of voices behind her as she walked away. Her hand went to her throbbing face, which she had just begun to feel again. She made her way to the place where she had been sleeping before the attack. Her possessions lay in a clutter among those of her warder, the neat bundles ripped apart and scattered. Beneath her foot she felt something hard and square. Stooping down, she discovered her handbook. Inside the begrimed leather of its binding, she found that the illuminated *æsc* and the maxim in Father John's hand had taken no damage. In the moonlight which now bathed the camp, Flæd stared at the writing. *A woman must shine, cherished among her people . . . she must know what is wise. . . .*

A movement caught her eye. Closing the book, Flæd took a step forward. A tiny shadow lifted from the grass, and then another—wisps caught on the little night wind. There in front of Flæd lay the remnants of her sisters' gift. Flæd watched the last downy bits of bulrush seed blow away from the torn cloth. Then, slowly, she shrank down to the ground and dropped her book. Curling onto her side, she laid her cheek on the tattered fabric and brought both hands up to cover her mouth, stifling sobs which would not stop.

21

Fortune's Wheel

WITH A LOUD CRACKING SOUND THE LEAD WAGON LURCHED TO
one side. A splintered end of the front axle tore through the
wagon bed, and Flæd and the driver were thrown into the
mud as the horses plunged and the wagon twisted.

"Cut the traces!" the driver screamed, scrambling to
reach the harness with his own knife. In a few moments the
horses were freed, and Flæd and the thanes gathered around
the ruined wagon.

"Too heavy in this mud," said the retainer who had argued the night before and whose name, Flæd had learned,
was Osric. He kicked a wheel sunk to its hub in muck, and
looked around them in disgust. "We still don't know where
we are, and now we can't move."

"Can we save it?" Flæd asked the driver, who was emerging from beneath the wreck. The man spread his hands.

"In the burgh maybe, a wheelwright with his tools could.
I can't fix it here. The attack must have damaged it." Flæd bit
her lip, looking behind them where the other wagon waited.

The five prisoners and the retainers assigned to guard them sat gloomily in the bed. Oat and Apple slouched in harness. All the surviving goods of her dowry had been loaded into this lead wagon, along with one other large, muffled bundle—Flæd's mind still shied away from this terrible proof that her warder was lost to her.

But she would have to face it now. Somewhere in the woods around them, enemies could still be coming to overtake them. Her party would now have to shift the burden of passengers and cargo, trying not to lose even more time. Flæd spoke quietly to the driver—could the harness be altered for four horses? A new wagon tongue, he hemmed, some makeshift fastenings . . . She left him to it, and picked her way through the mud to stand in front of Osric.

"We need the prisoners to load the other wagon with the most valuable of these goods. You speak their language—you could direct them."

"Yes, Lady. But who will direct us out of this forsaken place?" he said angrily. "Does any one of us know this country?"

"We travel east to Lunden," Flæd said in a level tone. "We will follow the course of the river."

"When we find it again," Osric muttered, squinting into the woods around them. He glimpsed Flæd's sober countenance, and jerked up sullenly. "All right. I will talk to the prisoners."

"I thank you," Flæd said without visible emotion. An inner part of her, which she was determined to show no one, was humming with nervous anger. She hated this vile sparring with Osric, who seemed to be the spokesman for most of the remaining West Saxon party. But she was forced to deal with him—her party needed every one of its remaining fighters. With the prisoners and several of the thanes now forced to go on foot, their journey would take far longer than the day's travel they had planned. And the longer it took to reach Lunden, the more danger they faced.

When they had set out at dawn, she had told herself with as much certainty as she could muster that they would see Ethelred in a matter of hours. Now as her men began to unload the ruined wagon, Flæd looked back at the path they had followed. Silently she admitted that there was no way to tell exactly how close they were to Lunden. What if they wandered for days before they found the way?

Flæd could already see a terrible choice before her. The crowded remaining wagon and the doubtful length of their journey . . . nearer to Lunden, they might have been able to send Ethelred's men back to bring her warder's body. But now, out of room in their single wagon, unsure of their location, and not knowing when anyone might be able to return to this spot, they needed to find a way to show respect for Red. Flæd turned to Dunstan, the young retainer who had come to find her after the attack.

"Gather the men who can be spared from the work here," she told him, "and please"—her tongue stumbled over the words—"bring . . . the body of the Mercian envoy."

They buried Red in a sorry grave dug with knives and hands, and piled a cairn of stones above him when they had finished. With filthy, scraped fingers Flæd placed her last stone, and knelt looking at the resting place she had made for her guardian. She had wanted to bring his body to Lunden, so that his death could be remembered with honor and ceremony. Now she would only be able to tell Ethelred what his splendid thane had done to save her. It seemed a poor gesture in return for Red's noble care.

As the others made their way back to the wagons, Flæd stayed for a moment. No one will see me, she thought as she laid her palm on the earth beside her warder's grave. A hot tear fell onto her hand and ran between her fingers into the dust, then another. She had never truly merited his loyalty. Perhaps, she told herself harshly, that was why she had lost the one friend she would have had in Mercia.

When Flæd left the little clearing, her face was scrubbed dry, her mouth set in an unmoving line. On her way she stooped one more time to pick up two dull metal rings, one smaller, and one larger, which had been carefully set aside.

With almost half its members walking, the West Saxon party travelled even more slowly, halting several times to send out riders in search of the river. Flæd had gone to check her horses' improvised harness during one of these stops, and as she came around the wagon she heard low snatches of venomous speech.

". . . never make it to Lunden before week's end at this rate . . . stupid to take prisoners, should have killed them all after what they said about the envoy . . . call her 'Lady,' but curse me if I'll follow her to my death . . . not her place to lead us."

Flæd shrank back beside the wagon where the cluster of thanes could not see her. The voice was Osric's, but the circle of listeners around him had included three battle-hardened thanes, and even one of the young retainers who had supported her last night. They're just listening; it doesn't mean they're all with him, she told herself. But it was ugly and troubling to hear such things. She hadn't even been sure she *was* their leader. I'm a person to blame when things go badly, she thought with an acid smile—that is the pleasure of my first command.

Late that afternoon they moved a little further in what they thought was the direction of the river. As night fell, two more scouts were sent to find what they could before morning, and the rest of the company drearily made camp.

Flæd had seen to her horses, and then found a place to make her bed in the growing darkness. There would be no fire on this warm night, and the party would sleep early, and rise at first light. Dunstan had arranged his things as close to her as politeness would allow, and she noted the seriousness with which the young man approached the task of guarding her. He will carry out his promise to my warder, she thought, whether I want his company or not. Anyhow, tonight she felt glad to have him nearby. The two of them ate their ration of food and drank water from a spring they had passed earlier that day.

"My father says that Lady Fortune's wheel is like the wheels of our wagons," Flæd spoke first, softly, so that only Dunstan could hear her. "And he says that people are arranged all around it—on the spokes, on the rim, close to the hub. Some of us on the outside, we ride Fortune roughly, sometimes down into the mud."

"Where we break an axle now and then, eh, Lady?" Dunstan said ruefully.

"And sometimes the rough ride takes us up into happiness and prosperity. It changes again and again. But other people," she said, pulling her blankets closer, "ride the spokes closer to the hub, and things are never so low, or so high for them."

"What's at the center, Lady?"

"At the center is God, I think," she replied, gingerly touching her still-swollen jaw. "All my life I have ridden amid the spokes, and now suddenly I am on the rim."

"And in the mud, you are guessing?" Dunstan said, leaning to put his hand over hers. She nodded.

"There is ill will in our company."

"They all have a duty to protect you."

"That is the only reason they have stayed with me this far,

and it will not keep them here if worse trouble comes. I want to stay alive—I want us all to stay alive." She stood, straightening her clothes. "I should go talk to the others." He nodded, getting up to come with her, as she had hoped he would.

Four faces stared back at her on the other side of the campsite. The two young men who she had thought might take her part again were not present. They had been assigned to watch the prisoners tonight. She would have liked to see the face of the old limping thane who had supported her the night before, but he had been chosen to ride for help—not to Lunden, as Flæd had suggested, but back to her father's burgh. Ethelred was closer and would come sooner, she had argued. The aldorman knew they were coming, Osric had shot back, and would already be searching for them. They would double their chances by sending a messenger to Alfred, he promised his companions.

That had been her hostile conversation with these men this morning, she thought with a sinking feeling. What would they say to her after the day's latest disasters? She drew a long breath.

"If our scouts come back without finding the river," she began bluntly, "what should we do?"

"Several things, Lady," Osric growled from the middle of the gathering. "Rid ourselves of the prisoners, first of all, then find ourselves some more horses, then get home."

"We need more horses," Flæd agreed in a guarded tone. "But as for the men we captured, Ethelred will want to question them." She thought of what she had heard in her father's council room. What should she tell these retainers about the rising threat at the western border? "Ethelred and my father," she said, choosing her words with care, "suspect that the Danes and northern Welshmen have formed an alliance. Our prisoners might know something about that."

"Our prisoners are Danish," Osric snorted, "stupid as oxen. I promise you none of them could speak a word of Welsh." Flæd felt surprised. She had kept away from the captured raiders, not wanting to look at the men who had cut her warder down. Now she realized she knew almost nothing about them.

"Have they told you where they come from?"

"They won't say much"—Osric shook his head—"but they're straight from the north, I'd guess, from the Danelaw around Eoforwic, maybe. If you want them to talk, Lady, we could make them talk." He smiled grimly. "I learned my share of tricks with a knife in the wars."

"What good would that do?" Flæd demanded. "We can't let them go—if they didn't attack us themselves, they'd bring other raiders down on us."

"I don't suggest we let them go." Osric's voice was flat and dangerous. The men around him murmured. Flæd couldn't tell if these were sounds of outrage or of approval.

"We are King Alfred's men," a voice called out beside her. "He offers his enemies an honorable death in battle, and fair treatment after capture, not murder. We will not kill men held helpless among us." Flæd had almost forgotten Dunstan was there. Grateful for his words, she swallowed nervously, but she did not break off the level gaze she had aimed at Osric.

"Ethelred must question these men," she said as forcefully as she could. "The Danes will come with us in the morning. If our scouts have found no sign of the river, we will look for a farmstead, where a churl may sell us food and horses. Is this acceptable to you?" There was no reply. With effort Flæd maintained the firm set of her mouth as she surveyed the firelit faces a last time. "We will see what morning brings," she ended, knowing that the words sounded as feeble as she felt.

"They are not with us," Flæd muttered as she and Dunstan settled down for the night.

"They are afraid, but they will see that your plan is right," Dunstan said with assurance. Flæd pillowed her head on her arm, wishing she could believe him. Fortune's wheel, she remembered. I am still down in the mud.

The man who came running in the grey light of dawn forgot to hail them, and Dunstan was on his feet with drawn sword before the thane could gasp out his first words.

"They're gone, Lady!"

"Who is gone?" Dunstan gripped the retainer's arm as Flæd struggled up.

"The prisoners, Lady"—the thane twisted around—"and Osric is dead."

22

Dead Letters

"GET UP!" FLÆD STRODE WITH DUNSTAN AMONG THE MEN, rousting them out of their sleep. She grasped another man's shoulder to shake him awake and drew a sharp breath of surprise as one of the two young retainers turned his bleary face to her. "Why are you here?" she demanded. "Why did you leave the prisoners?"

"Osric took our watch," came his mumbled reply, "told us to get some rest." So this was how it had begun, Flæd realized.

"Get your things together," she told him, moving on to the next sleeper. "We have to leave."

With the man who had brought the bad news following along behind them, Flæd and Dunstan went to view the wagon where the prisoners had been kept.

"They were bound up, and then tied to the wheels," the man was saying. "We only ever let one free at a time to eat or piss."

"How did you know to check them this morning?" Flæd said, confronting the retainer. "Was it your watch?"

"No, Lady," the man whispered. "I knew he was going to them."

"You mean Osric?"

He nodded, eyes on his boots. "He went to find out whatever it was you said the king and the alderman needed to know. He said it was the only way to get you safe to Lunden." Flæd let out a groan. Osric had thought to serve her best by going against her, and he had paid an appalling price. Beneath the wagon they found his body where it had rolled into a pool of bloody mud.

"Bashed on the head with a rock," Dunstan said quietly, "then throat cut with his own knife for good measure." Flæd could not look at the dead thane. She stood up beside the wagon, sickened by the violence which Osric had planned, the violence done to him. She tried to remind herself that he had chosen to untie at least one of the prisoners, probably to torture him, but the thought did not make Osric's own end seem less gruesome.

"Do we know when they escaped?" she asked.

"He sent the others back to sleep just after it was fully dark," the cringing thane replied. "I think they have been gone for many hours. They took no horses." Flæd tried to put these facts together. The raiders had taken no horses. Why? For stealth, perhaps—to insure that the rest of the camp slept through their departure. And maybe because they didn't have far to go. Flæd grabbed Dunstan's arm, suddenly very frightened.

"I think they're coming back," she said to him, "and leading the others to us. We have to leave this place, now!"

The camp was in disarray when Flæd and the two thanes returned. No horses had been saddled yet, and an argument had broken out among the men standing amid their hastily bundled belongings.

"Is it true," one man shouted when he saw her, "that Osric is dead, and we leave without giving him burial, or showing some other form of respect for a fallen comrade's body?" Flæd looked at her little band. She had felt strange about giving orders to fighters far older than she, and this morning's events had bewildered her with blood and the threat of a new attack. But in this moment, looking at the shouting thane's face, she forgot her inadequacy. She felt anger at these men's heedless ways, their squabbling approach to each new problem. They had once been united in their respect for Red, she felt sure, but nothing held them together now, and they would probably die very soon unless that changed.

"Your friend is dead," she said in a freezing voice. "He has brought terrible danger to all of us. Stay and bury him if you like. You will not finish before the raiders cut you down." The voices of the men sprang up again like flames over dry wood, and she shook her head in frustration. "You have another choice," she said loudly, and the company quieted again. "You can follow me, the king's daughter whom you pledged to escort and protect. We will keep moving east, as fast as we can. We will leave now."

Flæd turned and half ran to her picketed horses. Would anyone help her hitch them to the wagon? She didn't know, and there was not time to wait and find out. Chirping to the big animals as she gathered up their picket ropes, she jogged with them to the wagon where their harness lay.

And then Dunstan was there beside her with her bedding rolled and tied. A wagon driver took the horses and led them to their places. The sound of hoofbeats and running feet rose up around her as the company gathered. Flæd let out the breath she had not known she was holding. She took her place on the wagon box, ready to order them forward.

"Lady," Dunstan called out from the back of his restless horse, "our scouts!" Looking southward where he pointed, Flæd saw the two riders urging their exhausted mounts toward the company.

"The river," one shouted as soon as he was near enough to be heard, "we reached it! And a fresh camp—we think Ethelred's party stayed there!" Flæd's heart, which had beat faster and faster as her men gathered around her, felt all at once as if it would burst her chest. They had found the river, and the way to Lunden!

"Take us there," she said, trying to show the calm face of a dignified leader. The wagon jerked forward and she caught her balance. *We are out of the mud!*

Ethelred's campsite lay less than two hours' journey away. Despite the horrors of the last two days, Flæd's spirits kept rising as they rode into the meadow where the sound of the river filled the air like a great, whispering voice. The Mercians had stayed here less than two weeks ago. Now the West Saxons would be able to follow the marks of feet and hooves, or go along the river if they lost the track. They must not be far from Lunden. *We will not stop again for sleep,* Flæd vowed. *The raiders might be very close.*

But they would take time to get water from the river, and let the horses who had carried the scouts and the ones who had to bear two riders breathe and drink a little. The company dismounted to lead their horses to the water, and Flæd slung waterskins around her neck for the four horses in harness and went with Dunstan along the riverbank.

The track they followed wound back to the north and west, bringing them up close to a little hill before it sloped back down to a wide bar beside the river where Dunstan's horse could stand and Flæd could fill her leather pouches. Halfway down the embankment Dunstan's mare began to toss her head. Then she pulled back so violently that the bit cut her mouth, and bloody foam sprayed over them.

"What is it?" Flæd asked as the thane tried to soothe the horse who was dancing backward now, and trying to bolt.

"She sees something she doesn't like," Dunstan grunted as the horse jerked his arm again. "Or smells it," he said, blowing into the horse's nostrils to calm her.

Then Flæd smelled what the horse had: a sweet carrion odor. She paced ahead five wary steps and stopped with a jerk. There lay the bodies of a man and a horse. Two arrows had pierced them with extreme precision—the horse through the eye, and the man through the neck. They had been dead for some time.

"Dunstan!" she hissed. Flæd heard her retainer say a few more soft words as he tethered his horse to a tree, and then he came running to join her. "I know this man," she told him, swallowing against the bile that rose in her throat. "He was Cenwulf, the Mercian emissary who brought my father news from the Welsh border, and then rode with Ethelred."

"The alderman would have sent searchers for a trusted messenger, if he had gone missing," Dunstan said, going carefully forward to take a look at the dead man.

"Unless Ethelred himself had sent another message with this man," Flæd returned, still trying not to retch, "not to Lunden—somewhere else."

"There is something here. . . ." Dunstan was saying as he reached gingerly beneath the man's leather breastplate. He drew out a roll of parchment, the edge of which was crusted with old blood. Together he and Flæd spread it out on the ground.

To Alfred, Lord of the West Saxons and King of the
English People, Ethelred, Chief Aldorman of Mercia,
sends greetings and warning. A raiding party has struck
our camp. Lady Æthelflæd must not travel before the
attackers are discovered and destroyed. We will look
west for their source after we bring our wounded to
Lunden. I write in haste.

The scribbled words ended in a clumsy dribble of wax
which showed the imprint of Ethelred's seal. Flæd covered
her face with a hand to ward off the horrid scent of decay,
and to control the alarm rising quickly in her. These words
written by Ethelred had lain here in Cenwulf's bosom, lost
and unread, every letter of the message as dead as the messenger himself. She and her men should not have come—
Ethelred had tried to stop them.

"Let's go back to the others." She rose and turned back to
stare along the way that they had come. Their situation was
even worse now, she realized. No party from Lunden would
be riding to their aid. Ethelred had said he would look to the
west for invaders, as the council with Alfred had taught him
to do. And thinking his message had halted their party, he
would believe the king's daughter to be safe in Wessex, not
wandering in Mercia. If only her men had agreed to send a
messenger ahead to Ethelred instead of back to Alfred, Flæd
agonized. If only she had marshalled their respect sooner.

Flæd and her retainer had begun to plod up the bank

when they heard the first shouts coming from the site of Ethelred's camp. Then a scream cut the air. Flæd started to run, but Dunstan's strides were longer, and he beat her to the horse. He clambered into the saddle, pulling Flæd up behind him.

Her men were reining the horses frantically at the edge of the meadow, shouting for Dunstan and Flæd as the two of them crashed into the open. A horse ran riderless across the clearing, and two bodies slumped in the grass, bristling with arrows.

"Raiders!" shrieked the wagon driver as he saw Flæd and Dunstan charge up. Apple, Oat, and the other two horses in harness leaped forward as he gave them their heads, and with the five other mounts left to them, the surviving members of the West Saxon party streamed up into the hills.

23

Hunter and Hunted

WITH A DEADLY RAIN OF ARROWS THE RAIDERS WERE DRIVING them north, away from the river—somehow Flæd noticed this as she clung to Dunstan's belt and shoulder with straining fingers. Their attackers never seemed far away, although the momentary flash of a pale face and the movement of dark-clad forms was all Flæd could glimpse when she tried to look back.

"We can ride ahead, Lady!" Dunstan cried out over his shoulder. "My horse is faster than the wagon and the others!" Should the two of them speed on without her men? There had been something unaccountable about what had just happened in the meadow. Why had the raiders killed only two of her thanes while the entire company waited at their mercy, calling for her?

"No, stay back!" she screamed. The raiders had wanted *her*, she thought she understood. They had harassed and mangled her company to bring her running back to them. Now that she had appeared, her thanes would be killed without remorse—they had outlived their usefulness. The only way to save her men would be to help them outrun the enemy.

"Faster!" she yelled to her riders, whose speed had begun to slacken. We are too slow, Flæd despaired. But it appeared that somehow their lumbering progress was enough. The wagon creaked incessantly over the rough course they had chosen—every person or animal within half a mile must know exactly where they were. Still, there came no attack.

"Let me ride in the wagon," she gasped in Dunstan's ear, and the company slowed enough for her to slip off of Dunstan's horse and into the grasp of a thane riding in the wagon bed. They would have to turn south again if they were to reach Lunden, the only defended city any of them knew in this place.

"Can we get back to the river?" She gestured around the tense body of the driver, who threw a look over his shoulder at the wooded country they would have to cross again, and then sent his team toward a gap in the trees. The West Saxon riders swept around with them, and everyone began to pick up speed with the downhill journey.

"Ahh!" A retainer riding next to the wagon cried out in pain. Flæd's driver leaned back in consternation, sawing at the reins and almost bringing his horses to a stop before he sent them lunging back up the hill. The rider who had cried out reeled precariously in his saddle. He clung with one arm to his horse's neck as it turned with the others to race back onto higher ground. From his other shoulder protruded the pale shaft of an arrow. The raiders had caught up.

As the sun struggled across into the sky amid gathering clouds, Flæd and her men pressed north, and once again they seemed to outpace their pursuers. Every one of Flæd's bones seemed to ache from the constant jarring of the wagon ride. Her retainers had dragged the wounded thane into the wagon when he could no longer keep his seat on his own horse, and Flæd knew he would have to have a quiet resting place very soon, and hot water and herbs to clean and pack the wound. They should have seen some other settlement by now, she felt sure, some sign of human habitation along the twisting detour the raiders were forcing them to take. But if the raiders knew this countryside well, they might be able to steer the West Saxons away from any such dwelling places. Flæd began to think this was exactly what they had done.

She tried to ease her injured thane as the wagon bumped through another rough clearing. They were climbing again at a pitiful speed, and Flæd wondered how much longer the drooping horses would be able to drag their feet forward. At the end of their strength her company would have to make a final stand against the invisible attackers coming up behind them.

Was there nothing else the West Saxon party could do? Flæd stared at the countryside around them, trying to guess where her group might be headed. They had been driven north from the river. Before that they had travelled more than half of the distance south and east toward Lunden. Flæd closed her eyes, trying to picture the maps she had seen in her father's council room. Hadn't they spoken of Mercian defenses in this area? Of some difficulty with repairs? If her memory was correct, her men might not be far from a Mercian outpost loyal to Ethelred and Alfred.

She looked ahead of them. They had been skirting little rolling hills, and now one caught her eye—a mound in the distance, not quite on the course they had been forced to take. There was something unnatural about its contours. The hill leveled off near its crest, and then another tier, smaller than the first, completed the rise. This mound was bare and even on top, almost as if some giant being had cut and shaped it, like a child molding soft earth.

Flæd's eyes widened. Her mind suddenly filled with memories of her lessons from the great Chronicle, and of her talks with Red and Father John about the strategies of the Danish wars. A kind of ancient fortress—*"The earth from the encircling trench would be piled in the center until it made a hill which appeared flat at the summit . . . in times of war folk could bring their families and their beasts inside for safety. I believe your father has found and occupied several of these places, and is strengthening them for his own army's defense."* It was possible that this strange hill was an old earthwork defense, perhaps even one which her father had repaired. Her party might have a chance if they could reach it before they had to turn at bay.

"Driver." She pointed. "Turn toward that bare hill, if you can."

"What?" shouted one of the retainers in the wagon with her. "Do we take the advice of a girl when all our lives may be lost? Dunstan!"

"Lady?" Dunstan brought his horse up beside the wagon.

"I think I see a fortress, there," she said tensely, pointing again. "There might even be a garrison of men loyal to King Alfred—they could help us!" Squinting into the lowering mist, Dunstan saw the hill she meant. Without a word he sent his mount toward it, and the driver brought his team in line with the mound. The other riders altered course with the wagon as the first drops of rain began to fall.

Perhaps the rain helped them pull even further ahead of their enemies. Flæd's spent company seemed to be completely alone when it slithered onto a soaked path. The path widened as it approached the sloping embankment. This *is* an earthwork fortress, Flæd thought. They had reached the trench, from which ancient people had piled up soil and rock to make the mounded defense. Flæd could see that far more recently someone had thrown a flimsy wooden bridge across the gap, which was deeper than the height of a man, and at least as wide as two wagons with teams. Now she and her men struggled over the bridge and through a gap in the wall where a gate might once have stood. They had entered the circular fortress, and as far as she could see, Flæd realized with a sinking heart, it was deserted. Where were the defenders she had hoped for?

When all the horses and the wagon stood within the walls, the retainers led by Dunstan heaved the makeshift bridge onto its side and pulled it across the single entryway of the ancient stronghold. The horses hung their heads, winded and dripping as rain continued to drench them. Flæd covered her wounded man as best she could, and then crawled up the wall to join the rest of her group, who were now huddled atop the wall to see who would follow them.

On the bare hillside below a figure appeared, then another. In a few seconds fifteen men had emerged from the trees to stand staring at the mound where their quarry had fled like rabbits to a warren.

"We have been running from a band of men on foot," Dunstan said, disgusted.

"We ran because they killed two of our company"—Flæd shuddered—"and they could have killed more. Why didn't they?"

"They were moving us like sheep," a shivering thane offered, "shooting warning arrows from one side, then from another, as if they had someplace they wanted us to go. Not here, I'd wager, but someplace." The raiders were pointing at the fortress now. Flæd and her men watched as the small figures huddled together for a moment, then set out in their group toward the hill. At the base of the rise the group spread out again into a kind of half-circle, sweeping the terrain in search of the way Flæd and her men had taken. In all too short a time the enemy party had found fresh hoofprints and wheel ruts on the trail the West Saxons had used. The raiders started following the track up the hill.

"They're coming!" hissed one of the drivers.

"Nearly twice as many as our number!" another man groaned. "She said there'd be a garrison here," he said accusingly, "with armed men to help us, and a defended fortress. But there's nobody, just our company of seven men—one too badly wounded to rise—and a girl, trapped, and only a few sticks across the gate."

Flæd barely took note of her man's complaint. She was looking at the band of raiders, who were drawing nearer and nearer. She could see faces now—hard fighters, she thought to herself as she surveyed their scars and took in their pinched, mercenary expressions. Soon the trench with its steep sides would be all that separated the enemy from the pitiful barrier her people had thrown across the fortress entryway. The trench would not be enough to stop them.

"Best get to the horses," one man muttered. A few of the thanes turned with him to go down.

"Wait," Flæd said, looking along the wall to the entrance. "Can we stand at the top there?" she asked Dunstan, who eyed the ragged gateway dubiously.

"Two of us could, maybe," he said, waiting to hear what she would say next.

"Dunstan, and you"—she chose the man who had complained—"let's go around to the gate. You others, assemble below." She forced a note of authority into her voice, and it seemed to work.

Crawling to stay out of the raiders' sight, Flæd and her two men made their way along the wall. As they neared the gap, Flæd hung back and looked down to see how far the raiders had come. Five had slid to the bottom of the trench already, and one was scrabbling for a hold on the slope just below the opening.

"Hurry!" she breathed to her thanes, who were poised at the end of the crumbling rampart. "Push the loose stones over!" The two men threw their shoulders against the weak place, and scrambled back to crouch with her as the wet earth and rock rushed down. They heard the cries of the raiders, and when Flæd, Dunstan, and the other man cautiously looked over the sheltering ledge, they saw the members of the raiding party pulling their companions up out of the trench, backing off. One figure lay still in the ditch, half buried in the wreckage. Flæd turned her face away, feeling dazed. One enemy less to threaten her men. One fewer adversary in the battle to come.

The enemy band was clustered together again. Flæd held her breath, wondering what they would do next, wondering how she would find another way to discourage them. And then the raiders were leaving the open ground, fading back into the trees. Flæd began to breathe again, but she would not let herself relax. Some raiders would stay, she felt certain, to watch for any movement from the fortress. They know we're here, she thought, and they know we're tired. The others would rejoin a larger force nearby—she believed there must be others massing not far off to finish off her little group—and no one would be able to stop them the way she had thwarted that lone messenger running north two nights ago.

Two nights—it seemed far longer since that first attack. Flæd skittered down the embankment with her two thanes and met the others, who had gathered in the rain by the horses. She looked around at her bedraggled company. Two had fresh blood on their clothes from arrows which had grazed them in the meadow. The two-day-old gash on one driver's face had swollen unhealthily. Most looked at her with dull eyes, and she remembered, moving her stiff jaw, that she herself must have ugly bruises where Apple had kicked her chin. We don't look good to each other, she decided with an exhausted frown.

"The man in the wagon needs your help," she said to the driver who knew something of healing, the one who had tried to save Red. "The rest of us will try to find some shelter."

The fortress was very old—perhaps even older than Roman times, Flæd guessed—but it had been used much more recently. She could see signs of repair on the circular wall, and there was the new bridge which they had taken up

behind them. Someone had cleared out a few of the struc-
ture's rooms, which were cavelike hovels made of earth and
wood, built so that they leaned against the wall. Flæd and her
men huddled in these rooms until the rain stopped.

The more she saw of this place, the more certain Flæd felt
that this was one of the ancient fortresses which Alfred had
decided to use as part of his own defenses. But if this were
true, peasant workers as well as a group of armed fighters
should still be living here, finishing the repairs, and keeping
watch. Where were those people loyal to Alfred and Ethelred,
Flæd thought with bitter discouragement, slumped in a dirty
corner of the room where the driver was tending her
wounded man. Perhaps they had found another settlement,
or another fortress—some easier place to live. Disloyalty
and weakness had spoiled her father's fine plan.

It's not fair, Flæd thought—there should have been protection for us here. It felt even worse to know that at least
some of her men still blamed her for their predicament. I
sent the scouts to find the river and then followed them
there, the girl acknowledged. I let the raiders drive us here,
and I sent my men up into this fortress, where our enemies
can now keep us trapped until they decide what to do with
us. All Father John's instruction in history, all Red's teaching—what was it for? So that I could lead us here to die?

"It is our duty to keep ourselves sharp, or strong, to make
ourselves ready for whatever task comes to us." The edge on
the sword. Red's final lesson ran mockingly through her

mind. "*. . . if someone makes a choice for us, and we don't like it—maybe we even hate it . . .*" What if I hate my own choices, Flæd wondered with a bitter smile.

So she and her men would have to find a way to save themselves, she thought hopelessly as she got to her feet. She could hear the drip of the rain lessening, and as she stepped from foot to foot, forcing the blood back into her legs, she decided to search out Dunstan again. Together, she thought, stepping out of the little cell and calling his name, they would have to figure out what to do.

"Dunstan," she called again as she struggled around a pile of debris opposite the fort's entrance. Then she stopped, staring at the curve of the wall—a little deeper here, it marred the circle of the fortress with an irregularity.

"Lady?" Her dutiful thane strode to meet her.

"Get the others," she said almost frantically, "anyone fit enough to lift and carry. There's something here."

They uncovered the passageway just before dark. Flæd had made her men search these ruins of what she thought had once been stables, moving the rocks until they exposed the echoing hole she had hoped to find. With eight of them working to move the rubble, they were soon able to carry a torch into the space behind it, which proved broad enough for four men or two horses to walk abreast, and tall enough for a crouched rider to pass through.

Wind whipped around the hill, and they could hear it moaning over the tunnel's exit. It was a very old place—as old as the original defenses, Flæd guessed. Only a few paces further on they no longer needed the torch. Twilight filtered through branches growing thick and undisturbed over the passage's outlet. Shielding her face with one arm, Flæd pushed through the brush until she could worm her head and shoulders out into the open. She found herself on the opposite side of the hill from the fortress gate, well beyond the encircling trench. Father John had described such things to her when she had asked about the earthwork defenses of the Danish wars. The oldest ones, he told her, had been designed to give the fort's defenders a chance to leave a siege. Just as she had thought, this was another way out.

When she scuffled back into the tunnel she found her retainers clustered around one of the watchmen from the wall.

"Lady"—he stepped up to her—"we have seen firelight in the woods. It may be the enemy camp."

"Show me," Flæd said.

From atop the wall Flæd easily spotted the fires her men had seen—not even stars shone tonight from the sky filled with clouds, and apart from one or two little blazes lit by her own company inside the fortress for drying their gear and cooking, these were the only lights in the black landscape. There were far too many fires for this to be simply a camp set up by the fifteen raiders who had pursued them here. As Flæd had suspected, they had summoned a larger force.

Flæd climbed down and made her way to one of the West

Saxon campfires. She tried to consider all the things she and her men had discovered this evening—the hidden passageway out of the fort, the campsite where their enemies waited—she knew that finding these places could help them survive this predicament. But despite her efforts she could not see how. Instead, her mind began to fill with thoughts of her mother and father, Edward and the little children, her books, her corner in the scriptorium with Father John, and everything that had made up her quiet, happy life. What was she doing on a hill in this alien place, with a group of men who were half protecting her, half depending on her for protection? She was trying to stay alive so that she could marry a stranger—a man who, however worthy, did not seem worth what she had been forced to give up.

I miss Red, she thought miserably as she nursed a cup of hot water someone had put into her hands as she hunkered by the fire. More than anyone right at this moment, I miss Red. He wouldn't have let us run like witless animals from the raiders. He would know what we should do now, in these hours before the enemy hunts us down.

Flæd hid her face in the crook of her elbow. Red wouldn't want me to cry, she told herself. He would say, *"You will never be as strong as a larger man you meet in battle . . . you are smaller, quicker, and lighter . . . find a way to beat me."* She pictured Red in the meadow, waiting for her. *"If you can fool me, you'd fool them."*

Surprise. Stealth. Unbalancing her enemy. These were the

ways Red had taught her to save herself, and to win. Flæd tried to think. How could she surprise the enemy she faced now? An enemy who knew exactly where she was and how many men were with her? What would they expect her to do, and what could she do instead?

Flæd sat while her fire burned down to a ghostly flame wandering over red coals. In her mind a plan was forming, fashioned out of the day's latest discoveries and its early violence and, of all things, out of poetry. Could I really do such a thing? she asked herself as she mulled over one grisly possibility. When she finally stood up, she had decided. She saw Dunstan across the yard tending his horse, and went toward him. Her first challenge would be to convince Dunstan that she could stay alive if she carried out her plan. And after I convince Dunstan, she thought grimly, I must convince myself.

It would have been difficult for anyone to recognize the thing that emerged from the tunnel an hour later. Mud blackened its face. Leaves and twigs bristled from filthy hair and tattered clothes. Make me look like nothing human, Flæd had told them, like a monster wandering in from the night. Like a monster's mother, she thought to herself now, a monster woman standing at the edge of her pool.

Behind her came the sound of soft cursing as Dunstan wriggled through the branches to join her. She had instructed her men to clear the dead brush and leave only a screen of growth to hide the secret exit, but the job was not finished yet. Dunstan had insisted upon coming with her through the tunnel, and was now scratched by branches and bruised from his crawl over the tunnel's rubble. Dunstan was beginning to pay for his stubbornness, Flæd realized with a perverse glimmer of satisfaction.

"This is foolish, Lady, as I have said," he murmured as he reached her side and gazed at the distant campfires.

"We need to know what they are planning. And we need to weaken them in whatever way we can. I have the most woodcraft of any member of our party. Only I have a chance to go among them undiscovered," Flæd repeated firmly.

"I will watch from the edge of their camp," he insisted.

"And who will direct our men here?" she asked, trying one more time to make him stay behind.

"You will, Lady, when I bring you back safely."

Flæd could not blunt his determination, and so together they slipped into the trench, circling unseen to the entrance. The body of the fallen raider still lay where their rocks had struck him down. Flæd had been steeling herself for the task she would have to carry out when she reached the dead man. Now, gratefully, she felt Dunstan pulling her back. She waited while he knelt briefly beside the body and drew his sword. Afterward, carrying a new burden, the two of them followed the ditch back around the hill again. Almost invisibly they crept out and away from the fortress. There they waited motionless in the trees until they spotted the first sentry, and then two others.

It was not difficult, once they had seen these watchers, to pass them. It was easier still to find their way along a well-travelled path running between their hill fort and the camp-fires they had sighted. It was nearly impossible for Flæd, despite her brave words, to take the bundle and step away from Dunstan, beginning her solitary hunt through the camp. But she did.

24

Noble River

"MMMFF!" ÆTHELFLÆD SWALLOWED A YELP AS A ROCK DUG into her ribs. A pair of raiders was striding toward her as she cowered just off the path, and she held her breath, hoping they had not heard her little noise. Fool, she thought to herself, dreading discovery. But the two companions moved on.

Flæd's side ached as she eased herself up and scuttled toward the next campfire. She knew she had been extremely fortunate so far. Here in the heart of the raider's encampment, only one man had seen a small movement when she froze a second too late. He had made a sign which she recognized as a ward against evil (as if he thought me a demon, she remembered), then turned his back and hurried away. If he could have seen the thing I carry beneath this shapeless clothing, she thought, cringing at the bump of the package against her back, he might have shouted to the camp that a being of hell had come among them.

The fire she was approaching now had at least ten men around it—the largest single gathering of raiders she had seen in this camp of around four dozen. She positioned herself in the surrounding shadows, and began to listen.

Several speakers were engaged in an argument. They raised their voices, interrupting each other, and one man even began to shout until a movement at the edge of the group silenced them all. A person wearing a dark cloak stood up facing the raider who had shouted, beckoning him to come closer. Flæd gasped, then clamped a hand over her own mouth in fear of being heard, and in consternation at what she had seen.

The figure in the cloak was the man who had led her abduction in the spring. She stared at him as he leaned to address the raider he had summoned. Yes, there was the gaunt face she remembered. There were the dangerous eyes she had stared at when he spoke his few words of English.

Obeying his leader's gesture, the quarreling raider held out a sheet of parchment he had been clutching in his hand. The cloaked man jabbed at the page with one finger, saying something in a scornful voice that made the others around the fire laugh nervously. Flæd saw the raider open his mouth, preparing to respond as the cloaked man looked away indifferently.

Suddenly there was a flicker of metal, and the raider jerked his head to one side with a cry. He tottered before his leader, blood running from a gash beside his ear.

Like a beast sheathing its claws, the man in the cloak wiped his blade and returned the dagger to his belt. He did not speak again. With a groan the injured man blundered away.

Flæd stayed hidden as the bleeding raider passed her. When he had gone, she began to back away from the fire. She wanted to find Dunstan and tell him what she had seen, but she had come here to do more than gather information. *I have come like a creature of the fens, a shadow in the night, to bring confusion and fear upon my enemies. I have come to show them a sign of death.* On the path the raiders used, just beyond the firelight, Flæd placed the burden she and Dunstan had brought with them, and drew off the stained cloth they had used to wrap it. The head of the raider killed at the fortress gate rolled a little, half-opened eyes glinting, the raven crest of its helmet catching the distant light of the fire. The other Danes would know their comrade's face and his gear—the battle animal he had chosen for the helm's crest, its singular decoration. *We came among you,* this act would tell the raiders. *We will deal with you as we served your companion.* Flæd hardly felt like a person as she turned her face from the gory trophy meant to menace the raiders who had caused Red's death. *I am hate,* she thought. *I am vengeance. I am a monster woman, leaving a head at the edge of her pool.*

Flæd looked behind her. She could see no one approaching from any direction on the trail, but something pale shone on the ground. Silently she went to it. Reaching out her hand, she grasped at the white shape and found herself holding a piece of parchment spattered with drops of fresh blood. The injured raider had dropped the page his leader had thrust back at him.

In the shadows of the path Flæd could only make out a few shapes drawn on the crushed vellum. She folded it and tucked it into the pouch she had tied around her waist beneath her rags. After a moment's thought, she unsheathed the dagger hidden there and kept it in her hand as she moved swiftly back toward the place where she and Dunstan had entered the camp.

"Lady." She whipped around at the word spoken softly in her own language, but it was only Dunstan, who was emerging from a new hiding place close by.

"We agreed you would wait there," she hissed, pointing with her knife back to the spot where she had left him.

"We agreed you would not approach so many men at once," Dunstan countered. The two of them glared at each other, until Dunstan broke the silence. "You left our gift?" Flæd nodded, unwilling now to speak of it. "Then we will wait to hear how it is received." Together they stole through the trees to the outskirts of the camp.

"That man in the cloak, the one who is their leader," she said when they had reached a prudent distance, "I think . . ."

"I know him," both of them said at once, then stopped to stare at each other again.

"He led the men who took me in the spring," she told her thane.

"I last saw him one year ago, at the Danish surrender," Dunstan said. He glanced around, assuring himself that no one had followed. The two of them sat down in the darkness where a little moonlight came through the branches.

"He is one of Guthrum's men?" Flæd asked.

Dunstan nodded. "Once he was a *jarl*, a Danish noble-man with much the same rank as our aldorman Ethelred, and a person with great authority in the wars," the thane replied. "His name is Siward." Dunstan paused, his young face wrinkled with worry. "I will tell you what I know of him," he said at last.

"King Alfred had decreed that the Danes must be baptized as Christians when they pledged peace. Siward was forced to come with Guthrum's other generals, but at the place of surrender, he resisted. Two other Danes held him when the priest brought the holy water. He fought, screaming out in his own language and in the words he knew of ours. He cursed the English and Alfred, calling on his own gods for vengeance."

"He refused to submit?" Flæd asked.

"He did," Dunstan said, "and Guthrum was ashamed that one of his commanders would not obey him. He ordered that Siward be taken away and held, but that night the dissenter disappeared. The Danish guards, it was thought, felt sympathy for him."

"My father said in the council room that not all of Guthrum's people would be governed by the treaty," Flæd reflected.

"Siward would not," Dunstan agreed. "He hates your father, and it seems he has found others who share his feeling."

"Or perhaps he has bullied them into joining him," Flæd said, shaking her head. "I saw him punish one of his men for little more than raising his voice beside the fire. See what that raider dropped after Siward stuck him with a dagger." She pulled out the piece of parchment she had found and opened it where a beam of moonlight fell across her lap. Flæd could not read the characters she saw, but as she followed the wriggling line near the parchment's edge, she realized what she held in her hand.

"This is a map," she murmured. "Look! Here is the Welsh coast, the Humber River here, and beyond it the Danelaw." Her eye paused at what must be the border between Mercia and Wales. "Dunstan"—she pointed to several scattered markings—"these are the places where attackers struck the border outposts."

She tried to think. Why would Siward's raiders, lurking in the heart of Mercia, know anything about such distant assaults? Anxiously, Flæd surveyed the map another time. When she looked up, she thought she had found an answer.

"If these are all Siward's forces," she said slowly, "then he has sent only a few troops west, perhaps to confuse us. The main host waits here"—she touched the map in a place dark with the marks she thought must indicate raiding parties— "in the Danelaw, around Eoforwic, just as Osric guessed," she added in a faint voice.

"Weren't the attacks at the border made by Welshmen?" Dunstan asked skeptically.

"By riders who dressed like Welshmen, but who were larger men, like Danes, we were told," Flæd replied. "And the men who attacked me carried weapons made to look like the work of Welsh craftsmen, although the knife we took bore a Danish craftmark." Flæd gulped back sadness—her warder had shown them that mark. She tried to concentrate. "If Siward can remain hidden here in the country of his enemies, he is not a careless man. The Welsh weapons, the disturbance at the border—I think these things were meant to make my father and Ethelred look to the west."

"And if you disappear now," Dunstan joined in, beginning to understand, "your father and the aldorman will look west. They will take their troops and go west, while Siward brings his horde down from the north!"

The two of them fell silent, stricken by their discovery. It was Dunstan who finally spoke.

"Lady Æthelflæd, you must reach Lunden," he said emphatically, "nothing must prevent you. You and I may be able to reach the river tonight, alone—"

"Dunstan," she stopped him. It was the second time he had tried to convince her to leave the others, to protect her by asking her to desert the men. She could see the special need now for Ethelred and Alfred to know she was safe. But to disappear, leaving her people waiting for her with their preparations half-finished? "There must be something else we can—"

A cry from the camp silenced them, then more shouting. They could see raiders running along the pathway Flæd had followed, gathering near Siward's fire.

"They have found it," Dunstan muttered unnecessarily. The awful token Flæd had left seemed to be spreading fear through the camp, as they had hoped. "May Siward's men vex him now like a flock of sheep with one dead in their middle." He turned back to Flæd. "And we should go. Will you do what I have suggested?"

When Flæd and Dunstan left their hiding place in the wood, Flæd had a heavy feeling in her chest. She mulled over the compromise she had reached with Dunstan. What other choice did I have, she wondered as they stealthily approached the fort's secret entrance.

"We worried when you were gone so long, Lady," said the thane who waited for them inside. "We have made the preparations you ordered."

"Show me," Flæd told him. "And afterward, gather the rest of the men. We will discuss our plans, and then"—she pulled off her leather cap and rubbed her eyes—"some sleep."

The sound would always terrify her—that thud of boots in the night. *Flæd was dreaming of the room she shared*

*with her sisters in her father's burgh. Dove and Ælf laughed,
running around the wooden floor with small, pounding feet.
No, they were screaming, running away from something.*
She jerked awake as the heavy footsteps came closer, and
was already pulling her shirt of ring mail over her clothes
when he burst into the dirt-floored room where she had
gone to sleep.

"Lady!" The young retainer hissed in a strangled whisper.
"A new attack! They will breach the wall!" Æthelflæd considered this news as she jammed on her boots and reached
for her heavy leather cap. She issued two curt commands
which sent the man scurrying back down the corridor, and
then strode out after him looking for her horse.

We are not ready yet . . . not yet. A low noise of men and
horses filled the air as she emerged into the yard at the center of the fortress's defenses. She swung up onto Apple, already saddled for her, and quickly glanced around the torchlit
space. The enemy forces had chosen the least secure part of
the wall for their assault. Could her trick with the helmet
have brought on this early attack, she wondered with horror.
They had meant to unnerve and confuse their enemies, not
spur them into action! *The gate—by morning we might
have made it stronger.*

"How many outside?" she demanded.

"As many as forty, Lady," came the answer from Dunstan.
That must be nearly every one of Siward's men, judging
from what she had seen in their camp. Steadying her anxious

horse, she cast a rapid glance over the riders gathered around her—all eight of them looked haggard for lack of sleep, two were wounded, one badly enough that he sat bent with pain in his saddle. *Why won't he wait inside with the wagon and the other driver? He will be the first to die.* Without another word, she motioned toward the secret passageway opposite the place where the attackers had massed, and sent her own mount into the lead with a little leap.

Coming out of the tunnel ahead of her front riders, she pushed swiftly through the brush which choked the forgotten exit. She could still hear the shouts of the enemy, but now another rhythm had joined those sounds. . . .

With a shock she recognized the echo of a ram pounding against the fortress wall. She twisted in the saddle to look back—the half-ruined defenses could not possibly withstand such an assault for more than a few blows. *The driver who stayed inside, will he be ready? Will any of it work as we planned?* Time, she thought blindly as she kicked her horse into a gallop, we've run out of time.

And they had. Flæd heard the old bridge they had used to block the entrance give way with a creaking and snapping of wood. She and her riders had all left their secret exit now, and were circling around to the other side of the fortress, where the path led up the hill to the main entrance. The girl leaned into the swerve of Apple's gallop as she and her riders burst onto the path. The horses slowed a little as they began to climb toward the gateway, where the enemy would have massed, and Flæd gathered her limbs to urge Apple forward. She could almost see the entrance of the fortress. Suddenly Dunstan was beside her, clutching at her horse's bridle.

"Lady," said her second in command in a strained undertone as he fought to calm their two horses while the rest of the company raced forward and passed them, "we agreed that you would not risk yourself in battle!" *But I brought this on all of you! I brought us here! I stirred the raiders like a nest of wasps! I should ride first to save us, or be punished!* But Dunstan was right, Æthelflæd forced herself to acknowledge, reining in her horse. They had agreed, yesterday, as he said. Remembering this did not make it any easier to stop, while her little band stormed into the fight.

"Go," she hissed. "I'll meet you when it is done." Dunstan wheeled and charged after the others. *I will meet you if any of you . . . if any of us live.*

Flæd turned Apple off the path, heading for the stone outcropping she and Dunstan had spoken of when he made her promise not to fight if the raiders attacked. Both of them remembered noticing a massive ridge of rock as they looked down from the top of the fortress. It jutted out of the ground just ten paces or so away from the main route up the hill, Dunstan had explained, and Flæd had nodded. She knew just the spot. It was surrounded by small trees and other growth, and Flæd and Dunstan had judged it a place where a horse and rider could stand unseen. At the same time, a person hiding there could stay close to the path for a quick escape, if needed.

Sliding off her horse, Flæd led him into the shadow of the rocks where she had agreed to wait. Almost immediately the smell of smoke surrounded her. It had begun. She closed her eyes, picturing the scene inside the fortress.

The driver we left behind has set fire to the brush we piled in the entrance and splashed with my dowry mead. The raiders are burning and afraid—they forced their way into the middle of our flimsy barrier and met flames when they had expected a group of frightened thanes and a girl, easily taken. They panic. Some struggle back through the entrance, where my men are waiting to cut them down. Then—what? A more equal fight for her men, she hoped, still closing her eyes and hugging her arms around her body. A serious blow dealt to the Danish raiding party, and maybe survival for the West Saxons. Something better than helpless death like cornered animals.

Flæd listened to the rising sound of battle at the fortress. She still felt fear at these noises. *But those are my men, who followed my instructions to the end of their strength, who rode out wounded and tired and few, because I ordered it, and because they think they will save me.*

And I am useless, Flæd thought to herself. This could not have been what Red meant when he spoke of preparing herself, could it? Even when the world around her was not what she wanted, Red had said, it was her duty to remain polished, sharp, and strong—to be a shield at the ready, a point on the spear, the edge on the sword. Now she stood, ready in her place, and that place was in a shadow behind a rock.

Flæd cringed as an awful cry split the air above the shouts and clanging. *One of the raiders? One of my men, even Dunstan?* The sounds were so close, but there was no way to know unless she could see. Flæd beat her hand against the stones that hid her.

She waited, racked, as the fight went on, until at last she could bear it no longer. *I have to look.* With fumbling fingers she looped Apple's reins up close around a branch, and pushed his big body as close to the rocks as he would go. It would be very hard to spot him as long as he stayed still. She left her sword and shield hanging on the saddle, taking only her knife. They would catch in the undergrowth as she tried to go stealthily, and she was only going to look. She crept toward the path.

A hellish light glowed over the fortress walls—the brush was still burning inside. There was chaos at the gate, where the raiders had bridged the trench with rough poles. As she watched, a few of them stumbled out of the gate, coughing and struggling with the difficult footing of their bridge. Those who did not fall into the gap disappeared into the brawling mass of mounted fighters and men on foot at the other side of the ditch.

Flæd lay there on her belly, trying to make out her own

men in the moonlight, wondering if this was the time to flee to the river, as she and Dunstan had agreed she must. *Dunstan said it was my duty to save myself, that I must live to save Mercia and Wessex from Siward's pillaging.* But she stayed, and strained to see.

Someone was running. Flæd groped forward for a better view. Were her people in retreat? No, these looked like two raiders straggling off toward the woods. She turned back to the battle site. A small group of fighters had clustered together. They were stooped close to the ground and no longer raised their swords to meet the blows that flashed in the surrounding crowd. As Flæd watched, another man knelt with them, and another. What was happening? All around the battlefield weapons began to clatter to the ground—the kneeling men must be raiders, Flæd realized as their numbers surpassed the pitiful tally of her own thanes. Mercy, they were asking for mercy!

Æthelflæd's elation died away as she counted the figures standing and on horseback. Only five? There might have been nine if the driver who had stayed to light the fires had been able to join the skirmish. She thought there were at least a dozen kneeling raiders. Would they still submit when they saw that they had been routed by so few? Her men needed her—she could join them and seize one of the dropped swords. Careless of the branches that snapped around her, Flæd stood and ran into the road, heading up the hill.

Without warning her body collided with something dark and moving. Thrown backward, she hit the mud, thudding so hard it knocked the breath out of her. With a wheeze she forced a tiny amount of air into her lungs as the black shape heaved up off the road and came toward her. An excruciating grip closed upon her arm.

"Alfred's daughter," said a ravaged voice. A hand grasped Flæd's other arm, and she was yanked against the body of the figure who held her. The moon showed singed hair, hard eyes, a face twisted with the pain of a fresh burn across one cheek. An acrid smell of smoke rose from her captor's clothes. "My men say the spirits turn against them, but look, they smile on me."

Siward. Flæd kicked against his legs and tried to shove herself away from his chest. She cried out as the man wrenched her arms violently behind her.

"Quiet, Alfred's daughter," he rasped, bringing the burnt-hair stench of his face nearer. "I have you. Now that doesn't matter." He jerked his head to indicate the battle at the fort.

Flæd gave a little moan. She understood more than Siward realized. He would summon his northern forces while her father and Ethelred rode to Wales in search of her. Unless her band's battered survivors were able to bring this news to Lunden, Siward was right: Nothing about tonight's fight would make much difference.

"You have a horse," he said with a vicious tug that sent her to her knees. Bent down so that her face almost touched the mud, she nodded. "Show me," he ordered, allowing her to stand, but never releasing his hold. Flæd shuffled forward. Apple was only a few lengths away—she must think. With a show of reluctance she turned off the road and began to tromp through the brush. A limb slapped her in the face and she flinched aside, but Siward pulled her back in front of him. "Go," he said, propelling her onward.

As erratically as she could, Flæd wound her way toward Apple's hiding place. In the darkness she tried to choose the roughest footing and cross through the densest snarls of undergrowth, hoping Siward would falter. But his step remained sure. Soon they had almost reached her horse—she would have to try something else.

At the edge of a muddy hollow Flæd hesitated, blood pounding, and then deliberately stepped flat-footed onto the slick incline. With a whump she went down, pulling Siward with her, and rolling away as he lost his grip on her arms. On all fours she swarmed across the mud and into a patch of nettles on the other side, grabbing for her knife as she went. She had to get to the horse before him, she knew as she stood and began to run, never feeling the burn of the poison leaves. She did not know if the crashes she heard were the sounds of her own bolt through the wood or of Siward close behind her.

There was Apple, dancing and jerking against his knotted reins. She flung herself at the horse's head to cut him free, but a great blow from behind knocked her off her feet.

Siward panted, uttering harsh syllables which might have been curses in his own language. Flæd clawed with her free hand to reach her horse's gear, but it was no use—her sword and shield hung on the other side of the saddle. Siward's weight bore her down again. He spoke in a quiet voice. "Your horse, your clothes will prove to your *father*"—he spat the word with hatred—"that I have you. Why should I take you alive?"

"Dunstan!" Flæd screamed, but the word was forced back into her mouth by the Dane's muffling hand. He brought his other hand up to cover her nose, pressing her head back into the slime of fallen leaves.

"No one will find your body," Siward whispered as Flæd writhed beneath him. A fragment of poetry—*the battle-strength of a woman was less than a male*—echoed crazily in Æthelflæd's mind as flashes of light and color flooded her vision. She was going to die here, and this man would live. *His Danes will ransack the countryside.* With a jolt of desperation she struggled harder. *They will raid Lunden.* She flailed, her new home with Ethelred disappearing in ruin. *They will assault Father's burgh where Mother, Edward, and the little ones will be waiting, left behind.* Howling against Siward's palm, Flæd gave a last great thrash and tore one of her arms free. With a motion Red had made her practice in every imaginable posture of combat, she brought up her knife and buried it between Siward's ribs.

✦ ✦ ✦

They found her sitting with her back against the rocks. Apple had snapped the branch and stood, head hanging, a little way off.

"Lady Æthelflæd." Dunstan crouched in front of her and offered his hand, but dropped it when she recoiled. He looked at the body of the Danish leader which lay faceup, knife protruding from its side.

"Your blade," he said gently, turning back to her. "How did he find you, Lady?" Flæd said nothing. Dunstan leaned closer, searching for a response. "Are you hurt?" Flæd rolled her head to one side. "I should not have agreed to this plan." Dunstan's voice was grim. "I knew you would not go."

"I watched him," Flæd said, barely moving her lips.

"What, Lady?" Dunstan touched her arm, and when she did not pull away, began to check her limbs for soundness.

"I watched him die," she repeated, as if speaking to herself.

Her thane held out both hands now, and this time she let him help her rise. "She is wounded," he shouted to the others when he saw the terrible stains on her front, but Flæd shook her head.

"His blood," she whispered.

They had brought the wagon from its hiding place in the fortress, and there were new prisoners, and captured horses. Four of her men were injured—three could not ride—but the concentrated force and surprise of their attack had worked even more effectively than Flæd had hoped it would. All of the West Saxon band had lived.

Apple refused to carry Flæd in her gory clothes, so she climbed up beside the wagon driver, taking the seat they had given her on the day the journey began. It was three mornings ago, she had to remind herself, numbly counting the deaths that marked the days: Red and the raiders who died with him, Osric and the two thanes, along with the raider at the gate, and today Siward, dead by her hand.

The sky was light and clear when they reached the river. The riders let the horses wade in to cool their legs and drink a little. Ignoring the cold, Flæd walked into the water with them until the river, brown and clouded with the last day's rain, swirled around her waist. She felt it rush through her mail shirt and clothes to her skin. She untied her blood-stained cloak, the grey wool her mother had woven, and let it float away on the current. She had left her cap in the wagon, and now she unbound her hair and threw it over her head as she dipped down to let the gritty water scour her.

She was shivering and steaming in the morning air when she scrambled up beside the driver again. Someone handed her a blanket from the wagon bed. Dunstan reined his horse up beside them.

"My lady Æthelflæd," he said formally, "we follow the river?"

"We follow the river," she agreed, "to Lunden."

25

Lady of the Mercians

A HAND GRIPPED FLÆD'S ARM AS SHE SWAYED DANGEROUSLY on the wagon seat. With a little cry she opened her eyes. The daylight was fading, and in front of her loomed massive stone walls.

"Lunden, Lady Æthelflæd," the driver said softly beside her. From an arched passageway in the wall three riders emerged. Flæd signalled for her party to halt, and the mounted guard from the settlement stopped a short distance away.

"Say who you are, and why you have come!" one of the Mercian sentries shouted, his horse sidestepping nervously. Dunstan cleared his throat to call back, but Flæd stopped him with a shake of her head. She drew a deep breath.

"Æthelflæd, daughter of King Alfred, greets you," she said, trying to keep her voice from quavering. The sound of her words came echoing back from the rampart. Flæd saw the man move closer to his companions. They conferred, and then the spokesman rode forward again.

"Show us tokens to prove this," he called to her. Dunstan shifted angrily on the seat, and opened his mouth to reply, but again Flæd shook her head.

"If the aldorman and his party were attacked," she reminded him wearily, "the Mercians know they must be cautious with strangers." Flæd thought for a moment, and then reached into the pouch which hung at her belt. She drew out her handbook and opened it to the first words: KING ALFRED COMMANDED THAT I SHOULD BE MADE. Then she reached into the small space beneath her seat and took out the box which held her betrothal gifts. "Take these things to Ethelred," she called out to the sentries, handing the box and the book to one of her own riders, who proceeded slowly toward the group of Mercians. "He will know them."

Flæd watched as the three riders received the articles and disappeared through the passage in the wall. She looked around at the tired band she had brought with her from the camp the night before. The four retainers who could still ride had drawn up near her, slumped on mounts they had recovered after the skirmish. Some of the captured raiders sat bound in the bed of her wagon, shoulder to shoulder with her more seriously wounded thanes, and guarded by one of Flæd's men, whose eye had swollen shut above the gash on his face. He kept his sword unsheathed across his knees, regarding the Danes with grim purpose.

The West Saxon party had covered the remaining distance to Lunden in a day, encountering no further violence.

As they waited now outside the wall, Flæd wondered if it had been wise to give the golden gifts and the book to the sentries. She was sure Ethelred would recognize the rich things he had sent to Wessex for her betrothal celebration, but even an enemy might think to use such objects for deception. She hoped the chief aldorman had learned enough of her to know that the book at least must be her private possession, unlikely to be plundered. The Danes had destroyed entire libraries, she remembered reading in the Chronicle. At most, they would have ignored a little volume containing a few pages of writing they could not read.

"Lady." Dunstan touched her arm again, and pointed toward the wall. The three sentries were riding back toward them at a gallop, along with a new rider. *Four riders to our four.* Flæd felt her muscles tighten. Then she drew a breath of relief. The fourth rider was Ethelred.

Almost immediately, Flæd's comfort was shouldered aside by a crowd of old worries. All the feelings of uncertainty and resentment which had bred inside her through the months of her betrothal now rushed up again like a horde of enemies. *Who am I to Ethelred? Who is he to me?*

"It *is* Lady Æthelflæd!" she heard Ethelred shout to his guards as they came close enough to see each other's face clearly. He dismounted and came quickly to her, reaching to help her down from the wagon. Flæd was trembling. She had been calm since the river, where she had washed away Siward's blood, but now that listless peace had been broken.

"My lady," Ethelred said, grasping both of her hands in his when she stood on the ground, "we did not know you were coming. Our messenger . . ."

Flæd felt herself panicking. She had reached Lunden alive, and she had brought as many men with her as she could, but now those men would leave her, and she would stand beside Ethelred and be bound to him by a priest in front of all the people, and this man she did not know would take her to his bed. . . . Life and body—she had preserved her life and body, and now they would be his. Desperately, Flæd braced herself in Ethelred's firm grip. Ethelred had spoken of his messenger. "We found Cenwulf dead, with your message," she told him. Ethelred's face filled with dismay.

"This is terrible news—Cenwulf dead? He has been my surest emissary—we were certain that he and you were safe in Wessex. Lady Æthelflæd," Ethelred addressed her gravely, "your life has been in great danger. I am sure you did not understand the risks of your journey, but I must tell you now that we have sent a force of men to drive back the raiders who attacked us. They had found nothing yet, as of their last report. How did you avoid . . ." He trailed off, finally noticing the bound and sullen men behind her who could not be West Saxons.

"We have news of the enemies who struck your camp, I think." Flæd let the words stumble out, ignoring Ethelred's astonished look. "Here are prisoners"—she nodded toward the group of fettered men—"raiders from the border for you to question. A few of my own men are injured, and another man . . ." Flæd struggled with the words. "Another man is dead who was dear to you, and . . . and who was a friend to me. Three days ago we buried your envoy, who was my guardian." Flæd tried to keep her face sedate, but her lips still trembled. With fresh alarm the aldorman surveyed the members of her company, then brought his gaze back to her.

"My finest man," he said quietly, "a noble fighter. Mercia will receive this news with grief, and there is a certain person who will greet the news of my best retainer's death with even greater sorrow. Come into Lunden. Tell us how these things happened." Ethelred spoke to one of the sentries, who dismounted and took Flæd's place on the wagon seat. Ethelred boosted her onto the man's horse, and swung up on his own mount again. With a sign from the chief aldorman, the company headed in.

Inside, Flæd noticed through her haze of apprehension and fatigue that many people lingered in the streets, even at this late hour. Little knots of folk clustered together, speaking among themselves and pointing at the visitors as the West Saxon party and their escort passed. Flæd caught snatches of their conversation: ". . . the West Saxon king's daughter . . ." ". . . prisoners, see? They might be raiders—filthy Danes . . ." ". . . which one is she?" They had come out to see her, she realized. For the first time since the attack Flæd thought about how she must look. Her hair was bound into a ragged braid beneath her protective cap. Over her stained clothes she wore the mail shirt Red had given her, the dagger slung at her waist. Her hands were dirty, and her face must be covered with dust from the road. What must these people think of the Mercian governor's bride-to-be? What must Ethelred himself think?

Lunden was a larger place than the burgh where Flæd had spent her childhood, and she soon lost count of the turns they made among its streets. They must be nearing the center of the *tun*, she thought as Ethelred called for the party to halt once again.

"My sentries will hold your prisoners," he said to her, "and will show your men where to find food and care for their wounds. Will you come with me now?" Flæd nodded, and then hesitated a moment, looking anxiously over her shoulder. "Your people will not be far," Ethelred told her gently.

Still ill at ease, Flæd turned aside with Ethelred and one of his guards. The three of them approached a large stone building—the house where Ethelred lived, Flæd understood, *and where I have come to live with him.* The sentry took away their horses, and she and the Mercian aldorman went inside.

"You are very tired, Lady," Ethelred said. In the torchlit passageway where they stood Flæd looked at his face, still unfamiliar to her, though not that of an utter stranger. For a wretched moment she tried to remember what she had seen before in this face which had seemed pleasing. *His smiling banter with my father in the council room, and later in the hall. His quick delight when he discovered my trick after the race.* With less anxiety, she let her eyes trace the little lines around his mouth, the fine wrinkles that fanned across his temples after years of riding and fighting in all weathers. She could see that worry and kindness now shaped his broad features. "The bishop of Wiogoraceaster had already begun his journey to Lunden before our party was attacked," Ethelred was explaining. "He is here now in Lunden to wed us, but we will wait until you are ready."

"We must not wait," Flæd blurted out. *If we wait, how will my haste have been of any use? How would it show honor to Red, who lost his life bringing me safely to this marriage?* "The raiders tried to stop us on our way, and their leader plotted to defeat the alliance which protects Wessex and Mercia. But we didn't allow it—we didn't let him succeed, and I will not let Siward"—her voice cracked with urgency—"delay us any further." She fell silent, feeling far less certain than her words had sounded.

"*Siward?* The dissenter from Readingas?" Ethelred exclaimed. Sagging in front of him, Flæd nodded. He looked at her even more closely, then he sighed.

"As you wish, Lady," he said. "You must rest tonight. These people will show you to your rooms," he told her, indicating the serving women who had gathered near them, "and as you say, your thanes can give me your report, and spare you further disturbance this evening. But before you go, I must ask something more of you," he went on, shifting uneasily where he stood. "We must send word of these attacks to Alfred—the retainers who have come with you will carry the news with them when they return tomorrow, those who are well enough to travel. Your family will want assurance that you are safely here in Mercia. Will you write a letter to them, as you wrote to me, and say that you are well?"

The thought of her family and the familiar burgh made Flæd draw a quick breath of misery, but she looked up at Ethelred. "I will write to them tonight," she said, "if someone will bring ink and parchment to my quarters."

"Thank you," Ethelred said, but concern still showed on his face. "There is one other thing," he told her, taking her hand, "of which I spoke earlier. May the one who grieves for your warder come to see you tonight?"

For a moment it seemed too much. To speak of him, to bring that pain freshly to her mind yet again at the end of this day—I can't, she thought to herself. But he is not commanding me, he is asking, she realized. *She must be openhearted and generous,* Flæd remembered the maxim in her handbook. *She must know what is wise for both of them as rulers in the hall.* "Yes," she said at last. "Send them after I have changed clothes and washed."

"Æthelflæd," Ethelred said, and there was tenderness in the word, "welcome to Lunden." He kissed her carefully, as if he were afraid of disturbing some fine arrangement of her hair or dress. "Welcome to Mercia." Flæd felt his hand on her cheek, his mouth more gentle than the kiss he had offered after the race at her father's burgh. She was so tired that she felt herself leaning into his palm. Ethelred, she began to realize for the first time, was not merely a person to whom she must prove her value. *"He is a good man,"* Red had said, and Flæd could begin to see a kindness in him which might comfort her when she had need. Who else was there but Ethelred anymore, she thought to herself, and pulled back from him so that he would not see the tears that welled suddenly into her eyes.

In Flæd's room a little fire was burning on the hearth. The serving women who accompanied her took away the stained clothing she wore, and helped her wash the grime from her face and limbs. When she was dressed in a pale grey gown, with her hair neatly plaited and soft leather slippers on her feet, Flæd sent the women away. She found a place near her bed for the mail shirt, helmet, and dagger, which she had kept back. Several rushlamps burned in the room, and one cast its light over a small table and chair. In the bright circle shed by the flame, Flæd saw parchment and quills laid out for her use. On the corner of the table lay the little handbook and the box of betrothal gifts Flæd had sent to Ethelred from outside the wall.

What should she write to her family? Flæd went to the little table and touched the vellum. The thanes would give Alfred the details of the ambush, and would assure the king that his daughter had afterward come safely into the Mercian stronghold at Lunden. It was Flæd's duty to reassure them with her own words. But the sentences that came to her hardly seemed to express what had happened, or all that she had felt. *I have come to Ethelred's house ... Red sent me to hide during the attack ... their leader was Siward, who cursed the English at Readingas.* She needed to tell them that her new life had begun here, and that she had found comfort and protection. But in her mind she saw blood—the blood of an enemy who had meant to kill her, and that of a friend lying cold in the firelight.

There was a movement at her doorway, and Flæd looked up nervously to see the guard admitting a young woman. She was perhaps ten winters older than Flæd, and was dressed as plainly as the brown-clad serving women who had left her room a few minutes earlier. Aside from this, she bore little resemblance to the servants—a fact all the more striking because on her neck and wrist the scars of slave rings showed. She was not tall, but she walked and stood proudly. She waited now just inside the entrance with her head up and her back straight. Flæd peered more carefully at her visitor's face, and then went very still. She knew who this person must be.

"Will you come closer," she almost whispered. The young woman stepped to the center of the room, and Flæd could see that she was not mistaken. "He did not know if you were alive," she told the woman. "He said no one could tell him what had become of you or your sister."

"My sister did not live long after we were taken north," said the woman whose red hair shone above her drab gown. She spoke a little hesitantly, as if the English words formed awkwardly on her tongue. But her gaze was direct, almost defiant, despite her subdued voice.

"Your father saved my life," Flæd said to her. "I was not always a good companion to him, but he was generous and faithful. We tried to bring his body to Mercia for burial, but—" Flæd broke off, filled with remorse. She went to the corner where her knife belt lay, and untied a little bundle she had secured to it. "When I knew him," she said, unwrapping a piece of cloth which her sisters had once filled with seeds, "your father still wore his slave rings. On the day we made his grave, I could not let him wear them—I wanted him to rest with honor." She placed the cloth with its broken iron circles into the woman's hands. "I will miss him very much," she finished, swallowing painfully. For several seconds the red-haired young woman said nothing. When she began again, she might almost have been speaking to herself.

"The chief aldorman's spies freed me and brought me to Lunden only a week ago. Ethelred said my father would be coming from Wessex. I would have seen him again," she said bleakly. "I could have shown him my little girl, his grand-daughter. He would have loved her, even though her father was a Dane."

Flæd studied the familiar, square features of the young woman's face. Something lay beneath the austerity of her visitor's manner. Flæd felt a flash of pity as she realized that she was facing a person even more lonely than herself.

"Where will you go now?" she asked Red's daughter.

"Ethelred has recovered my father's lands, and has cared for them." The noblewoman studied the mark around her own wrist. "I have been a rich man's child, a Danish man's slave, and now I am wealthy again, and free." She raised her eyes. "I do not know what I will do," she said. "I need to see my family estate. Tomorrow I will go home, and take these with me." With great care she wrapped the rings again.

A thought had come to Flæd, and for a moment she was silent, wondering if she should say more to this person. The red-haired woman bowed in a graceful, practiced way and turned to go.

"Lady," Flæd said abruptly, "you and your daughter would be welcome in my household." The woman turned to stare at Flæd, who lowered her eyes, embarrassed now. "I— I am newly come to Mercia," Flæd explained. "At home I had my mother, my sisters, other women who kept our rooms and stayed with us. But I brought no women with me as companions."

For the first time a trace of a smile appeared on the woman's lips. "Thank you, Lady Æthelflæd," she said softly. "I will consider this on my journey." She bowed one more time, and proceeded to the doorway. Here she looked back once more. "My name is Edith," she said, "and my daughter is called Gytha."

When Edith had gone, Flæd stood, feeling her own loneliness creep back. She heard footsteps and voices approaching her room, and soon more servants appeared carrying armfuls of her belongings. After the serving people had left the room, Flæd inspected the little piles they had made. Atop a neat heap of her clothes she found the flat leather pouch that Edward had given her. She carried it to the little writing desk, where she spread out Edward's letter and sat looking again at the blotted letters of his short message. Finally she took up a quill, inked it, and began to write on a clean sheet.

To my brother Edward, son of Alfred, King of the West Saxons. I have reached Lunden, and tomorrow Ethelred and I will marry. Tonight I want to write something about our teacher and guardian, the Mercian envoy, who fell in battle on the journey. Tell our family that Red saved me. He preserved our father's retainers. He even saved my horses. I know he would be glad to be remembered as our protector.

Flæd looked at what she had written. Then she added one more sentence.

"And his people said that he was the gentlest and kindest of men, most considerate of his people, and eager to be remembered well."

She wondered if Edward would remember the last words of the great poem they had shared, its elegy for the monster slayer. Soon he would be able to read the poem for himself, she thought. Then, surely, he would understand what she had meant.

In the morning Flæd sat before a mirror of polished metal. She wore the bright red gown her mother had fashioned from the Wintanceaster cloth. Around her waist Flæd had fastened the belt of linked golden rings Ethelred had given her, and his betrothal necklace encircled her throat. A serving woman was twisting Flæd's brown hair into an intricate mass high on her head like a crown. Flæd watched as each coiled strand was secured with a jeweled pin. Then the woman settled Ethelred's third gift, the golden circlet, on Flæd's brow.

Flæd found that she was trembling. This morning the strangeness of everything that was happening to her seemed to strike with full force. Far from the place she knew as her home, she was on the verge of marrying a man who was almost as foreign to her as he had been on the day she first learned of their betrothal. Worst of all, hundreds of other Mercian strangers had gathered to greet their ruler's West Saxon bride. Flæd knew that they would find her unremarkable. *"Your message was most gladly received in Lunden,"* Ethelred had once told her. But surely the folk who thronged the streets could know little of the lady Æthelflæd, even if they had heard a messenger read the words of her letter. When at last they caught a glimpse of her, they would see a plain girl when they had hoped for someone like a queen.

The serving woman helped Flæd rise from her chair. She led her out of the room and along a stone passageway to the building's entrance, where Ethelred and his retainers were waiting. Flæd dragged her feet over the cold floor as she approached the group. Before she rose this morning the West Saxons healthy enough to ride had departed with her letter. Edith, the only Mercian she knew apart from Ethelred, had left Lunden for the present. The serving woman stepped aside and Flæd was left to stand alone before the aldorman's company. With a boldness she did not feel, she surveyed the crowd of unfamiliar thanes, and with a leap of surprise saw Dunstan standing there.

"You are glad to see the West Saxon thane," Ethelred observed, taking her hand. "Dunstan has asked if he may join our household as a member of your guard. If Alfred sends his approval, he is welcome to stay." Confused with gratitude, Flæd did not know what to do. At last she bowed to her friend, and Dunstan returned a low bow of his own.

"Now I must thank the person who discovered what none of Alfred's counsellors could see, and who ended Siward's treachery." Ethelred bent before Flæd. "Your men have told us how you brought them here. They would have chosen you to lead them home, if they could." Flæd looked directly at the man who would be her husband, and saw that he was regarding her not with solicitude, or amusement, or even surprise, but with respect. "Shall we go to meet the bishop of Wiogoraceaster?" Ethelred asked with a smile. Tightening her fingers where they rested in his large palm, Flæd nodded.

As Flæd walked beside the chief aldorman through the streets of Lunden, she felt the press of curious faces all around them. Mercian noble folk and craftspeople, servants and even slaves had come to see their leader wed the daughter of the great West Saxon king Alfred. The noise of their voices rose up on either side of the procession. Flæd kept her eyes straight ahead, feeling the blood come to her face with the shouting all around her. *They are mocking this red dress, laughing at these golden ornaments on an ordinary girl.* Flæd forced herself to keep walking, but she wanted to slip back and disappear into the group of nobles and guards who accompanied them. She squeezed her fingers around Ethelred's hand and closed her eyes for a moment, imagining her escape. She could dodge into some building as they passed. She would have to find other clothes, and then make a run for the stable, where Oat and Apple would be waiting, well fed and fit enough for a long journey. But where would she go? Home in disgrace? North, where her father's enemies with their strange tongue and customs held the land? Flæd closed her eyes more tightly as she felt tears burning their way to the surface. She could not run. Mercia was her home now.

". . . outnumbered them four to one, but she fought off the Danes, and brought the men the rest of the way herself, they say . . ."

"... killed their leader with her own hand!"

Flæd opened her eyes. She turned her head slightly, looking toward the voices she had overheard. She had expected skeptical, appraising stares from the Mercian throng all around her, but instead she saw smiling faces.

"... the thane betrayed by Burgred, he taught her, I'm told ..."

"... no wonder, for her mother is a Mercian, after all ..."

More snatches of conversation reached her ear, and now she looked openly at the scene surrounding them. Children ran alongside the wedding company, laughing and shouting. Men and women waved, cheering their leader and his bride. Flæd felt her spirits begin to lift, like a bird clinging to a bowed rush, poised to spring into the sky. Ethelred raised his free hand to the crowd as they went, and the happy noise increased.

Tentatively, Flæd raised her own hand to salute their wellwishers. "The lady!" several voices cried out. "Lady Æthelflæd!" Flæd felt a little smile start on her face. She was welcome, in spite of her fears. "Æthelflæd! Æthelflæd!" echoed all around her now, and then "Æthelflæd! Our lady! Lady of the Mercians!"

Historical Note

ÆTHELFLÆD OF MERCIA IS THE GREATEST WOMAN IN OLD
English military history. Although I have imagined this year
of her early life, we know much more about her accom-
plishments as a grown woman. Mercian records show that
the people of Mercia readily accepted Æthelflæd as Ethelred's
wife. In fact, she filled her role so skillfully that she was able
to assume her husband's duties when Ethelred became un-
well. After Ethelred's death when Æthelflæd was around
forty years of age, she continued to govern Mercia alone.
She was known as Lady of the Mercians, and she showed a
steady loyalty to her brother Edward, who had become king
when Alfred died in 899. Working together, Edward and
Æthelflæd built and restored fortresses, drove the Danish
invaders further into the north, and unified England south of
the Humber River under the rule of the West Saxon royal
house.

As Red explains to the girl Flæd in my story, Mercia had
at one time been a great kingdom governed by rulers as pow-

erful as Alfred himself. By the time of King Alfred's struggle against the Danes, Mercian independence had dwindled, practically disappearing when King Burgred fled from the Danes. During Æthelflæd's lifetime, however, Mercia seemed to regain some of its former strength. Æthelflæd's neighbors to the north—Scots and Picts, Angles and Britons, even Danish settlers in Northumbria—made alliances with her when they were threatened by Norwegian attackers. The Welsh kings, traditionally hostile toward Mercia, tolerated Æthelflæd's fortresses along their borders, and for the most part respected her military decisions.

In 918 Æthelflæd's personal direction of an important battle led her allies to victory over their common enemy the Norwegians. Then suddenly, in June of that same year, Æthelflæd died leaving just one child, a daughter named Ælfwyn. Perhaps Æthelflæd, who was always her brother's faithful partner, guessed that her death would signal the end of Mercia. King Edward let his niece Ælfwyn remain as Mercia's leader for only six months before he carried her off into Wessex and demanded the submission of all Mercians. Still, even after Mercia all but disappeared into Edward's holdings, Æthelflæd's reputation survived. In the memory of her own people she was the Lady of the Mercians, their last commander. And in Welsh and Irish records, which mark the passing of neither Alfred nor Edward, Æthelflæd of Mercia appears as *famosissima regina Saxonum*—"most renowned queen of the Saxons."

As I thought about the sort of girlhood Æthelflæd might have led, it seemed appropriate to make poetry and history a part of her upbringing. We know from Bishop Asser's *Life of Alfred* that the king educated all of his children, and that Alfred himself was a great reader and translator of books. You may have recognized that the poem which Flæd and Edward secretly share is *Beowulf,* the famous Old English epic. In her lessons with Father John, Flæd reads parts of the *Anglo-Saxon Chronicle,* which has survived in a number of manuscripts still read by today's scholars.

Flæd and Father John also know a number of Old English poems about strong women. *Elene,* the story of Saint Helen, who conquered Jerusalem and discovered the true cross, still exists in a tenth-century collection of poetry known as the Vercelli Book. The wrestling girl-saint Juliana, whom Flæd remembers as she thinks about her marriage to Ethelred, survives for us in another such collection called the Exeter Book. John mentions the apocryphal tale of Judith to Flæd, although the Old English version of this story was probably composed after Æthelflæd's death. We know that *Judith* existed in Latin from the fourth century on, and I like to think Flæd and her teacher might have encountered it in that language. It has the kind of plot a person like Æthelflæd would have enjoyed: A young woman leads Israel to victory over the Assyrians by slaying the enemy leader.

If these poems suggest brave deeds a king's daughter might attempt, the Old English maxims Flæd reads would have taught her the proper order of things, and the pattern of a well-lived life. The Exeter Book *Maxims* include a list of honorable behavior for ladies and lords, from which I took the words written in Flæd's handbook. And at the end of this same manuscript I found the maxim Red uses to encourage Flæd shortly before he dies. The poem begins with that sensible advice concerning shields, spears, and sharp-edged swords. It ends with words particularly appropriate for the Lady of the Mercians: "To the hardy person belongs endurance, to the bold a helmet, and always to a coward's soul the smallest reward."